T0300712

BAD SHEEP

THE GERMAN LIST

KATJA LANGE-MÜLLER

Bad Sheep

Translated by Simon Pare

Seagull
BOOKS

LONDON NEW YORK CALCUTTA

GOETHE
INSTITUT

This publication has been supported by
a grant from the Goethe-Institut India.

Seagull Books, 2024

First published in German as *Böse Schafe*
© Verlag Kiepenheuer & Witsch GmbH & Co. KG, Cologne, Germany, 2007

First published in English translation by Seagull Books, 2024
English translation © Simon Pare, 2024

ISBN 978 1 80309 401 4

British Library Cataloguing-in-Publication Data
A catalogue record for this book is available from the British Library

Typeset by Seagull Books, Calcutta, India
Printed and bound by WordsWorth India, New Delhi, India

Wobbly man,
wobbly man,
show me your legs.

I

We're lying on the two mattresses—not side by side, but nonetheless head by head. The artery over your temporal bone is pulsing against my cheek. Your hair's touching my nose but it doesn't tickle, though it does smell—of shampoo and of you. For several minutes or hours we haven't moved or said anything, taking shallow breaths. Your eyes are closed while mine gaze up at the open window framing nothing but a patch of cloudless sky that is neither bright nor dark. And if I could be bothered to puzzle over anything, then only whether it is dawn or dusk. I feel neither tired nor alert, neither heavy nor light; I don't need to smoke or eat, have a drink or go to the toilet. I don't long for distance, but feel no urge to hug you either. I'm free—not *to do anything*, but *from everything*—and yet I don't feel lonely . . .

This is the film that starts playing whenever I think of you, of us. I see that he and I both feature in it ('act' would be the wrong word), not as the woman I am now but as I used to be many years ago: younger, prettier and usually by your side.

I can't rewind this slightly faded and scratched film, only speed it up or drag it out, pause on my favourite scenes until the whole apparition dissolves because the phone or the postman rings again or because, undisturbed by further interruptions, I have washed up on the shores of sleep, closer today, farther away tomorrow.

The longer the film goes on, the less eventful it becomes, and perhaps this comparison with a stuttering movie or TV film isn't the best; perhaps the images that flicker one by one across my retina are rather part of a series of slightly blurry and therefore not dissimilar slides whose random and ever-changing order is controlled by my blinking, by when and how frequently my eyes shut, open, shut . . . The window-sized strip of cloudless, starless twilit sky; the mattresses with the bright-red sheets at the back of my room; our resting bodies; the two of us in the streets of Berlin; you at Joe's; me next to a box of old junk . . . now it is only the power of my own imagination that conjures up each individual picture and all of them together, justifying both the film and slide metaphors, were it not for the lingering scent of your hair, the sticky warmth of your temple and my cheek, our uncoordinated breathing and the promise of freedom in the carefreeness I felt then and feel again and again now. From the moment I first felt it, I have called it happiness—an intoxicatingly undramatic form of happiness that every memory of it brings flooding back.

~

While our film was running in real time, when someone *might* have photographed us, should I have enquired about your feelings, even though you usually acted as if they didn't interest even you? Were you actually capable of voicing your emotions, or did you simply find it easier to express such things physically, through glances and facial expressions and gestures, and occasionally with your cock? Did I ever dare ask you what lay behind that proud polar-bear look of yours, your calm indifference, your rare bouts of hyperactivity or love? If I wanted to find out, and I often did, then I would couch the relevant sentence in what people say is the most typical of all feminine queries: What are you thinking? Your even more concise and typically masculine answer was almost always: 'Nothing in particular.'

Sure, you weren't the most talkative type. You were taciturn and, more importantly, secretive. In your better moments you stuck to keywords, catchwords and punchlines, but you enjoyed reading fantasy novels, the thickest ones available. Words passed more easily into your eyes or from your hands than through your lips. You were a qualified typesetter, like me.

Wet my whistle last night for the first time in ages. It's great to be free with the sun so warm. But I have to leave my hobby alone, no messing around. The plan is to get some money, do some karate and look for my own place.

You're probably wondering why I'm quoting back at you what you wrote. Because the exercise book with your undated entries, which I never saw you with in all our time together, fell into my hands back then and I don't know whether—and if so, how well— you remember your eighty-nine sentences, which do not mention my name once and which I shall repeat to you nonetheless, or precisely for that reason, not chronologically but word for word, until I reach the end of our story.

Oh Harry, had this notebook ended up in someone else's hands and had they been curious enough to read it, they would never have guessed I'd ever been part of your life, which was mine and still is.

II

We met by accident. How else? Maybe fate did have something to do with it, since we could just as easily have missed each other. The day our paths crossed you weren't alone, and it was less than twelve months since I'd left where I'd grown up and stayed until my thirty-ninth year of life.

The scenes of that 17 April 1987, which affected me and—at least for the first few hours—maybe even you, are ingrained in my memory; and unlike the film or slide images of that mattress idyll, these scenes become sharper and more detailed with every viewing until now they almost look like writing before my eyes, as if they hadn't happened but were made up, the product of my powerfully nostalgic imagination.

The subway train had stopped above Nollendorfplatz. I'd got out and was once more glad to find the virtually deserted square laid out below me, lined with kebab stands, cafes, junk shops and florists, and glad that the day before I had only lost the small change from my cheap purse, and not the papers entitling an East German refugee who had entered the country via the Marienfelde reception camp to free public transport for a year. The spring sun was high in the sky, casting its dazzling, almost white light onto the square, which looked both innocent and rundown after the milder weather that had nonetheless brought no rain; I can still see that child, a slip of a girl in a fluorescent green anorak, entering my line of sight from the left, dragging her gym bag behind her and clearly deriving no pleasure from skiving off school.

I picked up a crumpled copy of today's issue of *Bingo BZ* from the ledge by the kiosk; probably left there by its previous owner because it wasn't their style to throw away something they'd paid for that was still of use . . . to someone like me, who liked reading the gossip and horror stories arranged in narrow columns beneath the crass, sometimes hilarious headlines.

As I flicked through the paper, a cigarette between my lips, I was heading towards my real destination, a bathtub in the flat of a social worker from Bavaria I fancied, when you and your mate came racing around the corner. You were acting strangely, boisterously, even crazily; like two chained-up dogs that broke loose, spent their first night under unfamiliar windows, yet to work up a proper appetite, though their gleaming pupils and the lunacy with which they were keeping each other's spirits up already hinted that they'd soon find and pay dearly for their freedom.

You were both handsome men: you, blue-eyed, pale and ash blond, the guy with you, olive-skinned with curly brown hair, shades and a small silver earring. The fact that the sweatshirts stretched taut across your broad shoulders most likely came from a charity shop escaped me at the time.

Although I was wearing no makeup and my stout body was draped in an article of clothing tellingly called a sack dress, I must have caught your eye, as the two of you had mine, because you stopped, you to my left and the other guy to my right.

'Hey, dollymouse, where you going?' you said so slowly and clearly that I thought for a second you'd already had three or four beers. But there was no sour whiff of alcohol on your breath, which I could smell because your face moved closer to mine as you spoke, but rather something that made me fancy a hot chocolate. I can't remember what I replied, but the word 'dollymouse' had the desired effect, especially as it brought it home to me that despite your irritatingly sluggish drawl as you strove to articulate, you could only be a Berliner, but not one who'd learnt to speak in the East. Before running into you two that day, I'd never met such a young and stereotypically street-wise fellow countryman— or rather, cityman—on this side of the Wall. The few people I'd got to know a bit better in the months after Marienfelde were, like the Bavarian with the bathtub, from southern Germany, and they regarded the 'independent political entity' as a kind of halfway house where you could study and therefore ignore, absolutely legally, the 'call to arms', or 'call of the flag' as we 'from the other side' referred to it. It took me a while to realize that these other people were not really all that different from me, an 'ex-Zoner', in that they too had fled from something, indeed that all the North, South, West and East Germans who'd run away here, along with the Turks, Italians, Greeks, Chinese, French, Americans and so forth, made up about half the population of the part of my city I hadn't been born in.

On the half-title page of the first book—a pirate edition—I bought with my first new money in a pub in early December 1986, I wrote:

Ever since I started walking through the western part of Berlin with the topography of the eastern half of the city in my mind,

I've known that this city really is *one*; the surviving houses on each side are as similar to one another as those added since the war. Berlin, East and West, reminds me of a last-minute gift, a box of department store chocolates left standing around for weeks because no one finds the contents particularly appetizing (they would say 'tasty' over here). Lying in the hollows of the moulded plastic liner, in which they are turning grey or to which they have returned unhappily with a nibble out of them, are, to the right, the bare pralines and, to the left, the gold-wrapped chocolates which, when peeled from their foil, look identical to the others— like two peas in a pod, one might say, if chocolates came in pods.

And on a calendar page for 14 March 1987 I'd used as a bookmark in that same volume, I had also noted the following two sentences:

I walk around, notice people and think: him and him and her and her . . . like me, they came here at some point to travel on or to depart again, at the very latest on the last train. But all the trains were long gone, and the last one never left. We've been in transit at the station ever since, and the station's name is West Berlin Zoologischer Garten.

'Me Harry, him Benno,' you said. A curtsey, not at all servile. And I'm Soya, I added—fairly reluctantly, as I feared that, as almost every time I introduced myself here in the West, they'd crack up laughing—'Soya? Really, and then what? Bean or sauce?' Only once did I try to explain that my mother, not I, was responsible for my first name because especially 'in the dark hours' of her 'first confinement', her mind had turned to her idol, 'the partisan Soya Kosmodemyanskaya, executed by the German fascists, who was to 'light my path through life like a guiding star'. Cue even greater merriment.

You, however, laughed no harder than you were laughing already. 'So, Soya,' you said, 'what's up? Shall we go for a hot chocolate?'

The way I returned your look must have demonstrated that you'd caught me out. How did you know what association the smell of your breath had stirred in me? I'd found your cockiness unsettling enough, but I found truly uncanny, as well as arousing, that someone could read my mind, especially as that someone was you. I flapped my arms, as if in doing so I might be able to take off or, at least signal, in my own shy fashion, that you were batty. Something about you attracted me, but at the same time something else warned me off—petty romantic inertia, though born of experience. Didn't all adventures, as my grandma once said, turn out to be bad ventures? What's more, Christoph's bathtub was waiting for me, and I didn't feel fresh enough for the faint swell of desire that was threatening to grip me and throw me at you. Or was it seeping into me through my belly button, like gas building up behind my diaphragm, expanding and gently lifting my spirits?

No, I said, I can't. I'm meeting someone.

'OK,' said your companion, who'd been silent up to this point but was obviously relieved, yanking your arm so roughly that the tired knitwear actually let out a faint lament, for you just stood there, as reluctant to be dragged away as I was to drag myself away. And yet I did what my conflicting emotions ordered me to do: I started walking, head twisted, not taking my eyes off you, shouting, Maybe later.

You pulled yourself free, ripping your sleeve like paper, and ran and caught up with me. 'All right, three o'clock on the dot, right here,' you snapped, your tone vaguely menacing, and you only stopped pursuing me when, having already barged into one lady, I decided to look where I was going again.

III

I'd met Christoph, the guy with the bathtub—an exceptionally large one—at the end of January in the Malibu on Winterfeldtplatz—every East German woman's dream bar—whose floor was ankle-deep in the finest, whitest sand. Between the tables there were fake palm trees and real *Ficus benjamina* trees, half-dead from cigarette smoke and lack of sunlight. Pink neon tubes shaped like giant flamingos arced across the black walls, and from the ceiling hung spherical lamps that cast a diffuse blue glow. It was mainly this blue lighting that attracted me to this bar because it made the hamburgers, spare ribs and baked potatoes you could order there look miserably bland. And so I never ate more of them than was absolutely necessary to avoid getting instantly wasted on the tiny cocktails which did, however, cost only half the normal price.

Christoph had sat down opposite me because all the other seats were taken. For about half an hour he nearly dislocated his neck peering at the door between the people streaming in and out, and emptying at breakneck speed the carafe of rosé that he'd been brought without ordering. When his expected companion, a certain Adrienne as I was soon to find out, didn't turn up, Christoph, whose handsome face had turned red from hurried drinking and perhaps anger, slammed a greasy leather wallet down next to his glass, stood up and swivelled on his own axis, scanning the room like a caterpillar that has reached the top of a blade of grass and doesn't know what to do next; but the scrawny, constantly hassled-looking waitress was nowhere to be seen.

An heirloom, I asked loudly, putting my fingers on the wallet. Christoph didn't make an anxious grab for his property, just grinned and replied as if I'd been trying to relieve him of something far worse than money: 'No, not *yet*—I'm still alive.'

He sat down again, beckoned to the waitress as soon as the toilet door had slammed shut behind her, offered to buy me a drink of my choice, ordered another carafe of rosé for himself and said, 'Pleased to meet you. I'm Christoph Merian the Bavarian.'

I told him who I was and where I came from, and then, as our respective roles required, we expressed our surprise for a while, he because I didn't like vodka and me because he stuck to this odd light-red wine even though the bar had a famous Munich beer on tap. Christoph outed himself as an Augsburger who'd grown up 'near Bertolt Brecht's family home' and come to Berlin six years ago to train as a teacher. It had soon 'bored him' though, in part because he didn't 'seriously intend' to 'tame children for a living'. He now helped out with a youth project called The Pump and had a weekend job that earned him a bit of money.

'How about you? What on earth made you turn your back on East Germany?' Christoph had the tact, unlike some, not to accuse me of 'betraying the socialist cause'. (Not that this hurt me much, for just as we'd dreamt of an alternative, I allowed you lot to entertain the opposite illusion.) Instead, he proposed I fill in for him at his weekend job from time to time when he needed to take care of something more important or visit his mother; and much later, as we staggered out of the Malibu, he also offered me use of his bathtub. 'Look,' Christoph said, slurring his words, 'here's a key to our flat. I brought it along for Adrienne, but she doesn't seem to want it any more. Come by whenever you like. We tend to leave home early and we're out a lot or else at our girlfriends'.'

Christoph gave my shoulder a feeble punch, uttered a 'ciao' that sounded like a miaow and then turned and strode away somewhat stiffly and bandy-legged, the gait of a sad but proud man shortly before the end of the night. When it had swallowed him up, I went my own way towards the Tiergarten, warming the key in my palm.

I'd rather have taken Christoph with me, and much rather have gone home with him, for the bathtub if nothing else. Since I'd been living among them, though, I'd consistently failed to charm any Western man of vaguely acceptable status. I was nothing special, I'll admit, but I did boast long legs, clean skin, an ample bosom and full lips. Back home in the East, where I'd still held some novelty and visitors were free to determine the degree of closeness or distance, some of our Western guests had been less picky. Two political science students, one from Marburg, the other from Bremen, had, one after the other, 'empirically tested' the 'erotic differences' between their 'brides' and those in the East with the 'aid' of my 'affections', as the guy from Bremen put it. I also remember a dentist from Heidelberg quite well; and a vasectomized American student of German literature who was so overjoyed and aroused by the sight of my stove that he couldn't help crying, 'Oh, this is crazy!' as his toes caressed the hot tiles. Also, some men who'd grown up with me or in other parts of our small country appreciated my straightforward manner and my indifference to any lasting attachment, especially as East German men tended to feel insecure around truly beautiful women as they were rumoured to want to be 'conquered and treated to this, that and the other'.

And now? I took great pains to emphasize my not-exactly-abundant charms with lipstick, fishnet tights and fancy bras under thin blouses. But despite the many evenings I hung around, bored, in pubs, nothing happened; nothing other than the occasional charitable or preachy interest in the—in any case truly unspectacular—circumstances of my 'soft landing' on the 'planet of real capitalism in the Teutopean solar system', for which Christoph had congratulated me during our first Malibu binge. And although I greeted his hackneyed quip with an offhand smile, I knew enough about Christoph's kind to wonder if he'd come up with this joke on his own or lifted it from a satirical magazine.

These friendly young men, so nonchalant-looking to the untrained eye, whose 'dress code' I learned to decipher before I even knew what those words meant, seemed to be wrapped in cling film. I could track their gazes, speak to them, hear them answering and breathing, but I couldn't really touch them. This I sensed whenever I put my hand on one of those men's hands and tried leaving it there for a while. It felt as if, no matter how much warmth their manicured, sinewy hands with their distinct, bulging veins radiated, they were still numb. Or was it my fingertips? The men seemed to feel this blockage too because they would withdraw their hands, usually discreetly and indeed carefully, while mine still longed for contact, my nervous system still waiting for something to happen that might quicken my pulse, raise my operating temperature and hone my sense of smell.

I reached Pallas-Athene-Strasse 12 as if on autopilot, opened the front door of the five-room, fourth-floor apartment in the second courtyard that Christoph shared with three friends and turned on the wide-mouthed brass tap full blast, allowing a disproportionately weak and irregular jet of water to trickle to the bottom of the deep, gently rounded bathtub which reminded me every time of the hospital chamber pots from when I was an auxiliary nurse, not only due to its shape and sound, but also because it would be at best a third full by the time the knackered thirty-litre gas boiler—mounted, fortunately, over the foot end of the bath—had finally emptied after about an hour. I generally used this hour to return this great favour by washing up, ironing shirts or making preparations for the soup that I liked to cook, nice and slowly, after my bath; for once, Christoph might come home before midnight or at least one of his flatmates Anton, Sven and Bruce might.

That Friday, however, I immediately took off my clothes and lay down, shivering, on the rust-flecked bottom of the bathtub. Not, however, so that the jet of water tumbling from a considerable height hit the sweet spot between my legs, since I was enjoying being in a hurry almost more than the mechanically induced orgasm to which I usually treated myself.

Towelling myself more or less dry, I sat down naked at the kitchen table, did my hair and my makeup with the aid of a foldaway mirror I'd found in the bathroom—and then forgot to put back because I was nervous, so nervous that my eyeliner was all wonky and my hastily hair-dryered, back-combed, pinned-up mane, sticky and stiff with too much hairspray, looked like a burst armchair, a frozen anthill, an abandoned crow's nest . . . I slipped back into the checked summer dress, which now struck me as being ludicrously premature, dug out a blue men's cardigan that would have fitted and suited Helmut Kohl, scribbled an apology for borrowing it on a slip of paper, slammed the front door behind me—and had time, nearly an hour, to ponder whether or not to keep my date with you.

I didn't chicken out though, probably because I didn't feel like tormenting myself later with sentimental speculation about what I might have missed, and also because I realized, or thought I realized in this kind of situation requiring a decision, that my mother was largely to blame for my 'habitual overconfidence', which she had often deplored and which had for ever divided us. Or were Soya Kosmodemyanskaya's misfortunes, apart from the geopolitical circumstances, not the result of her battles against the survival instinct so typical of humans and other creatures?!

Rather embarrassingly, I was already waiting outside the cafe when you arrived; the two of you, because once more you had Benno in tow. You gave me a look that made me think for a second that I'd forgotten it was my birthday whereas you hadn't. You presented me with a long-stemmed, somewhat wilted and virtually leafless and thornless rose, while hiding something in your other hand behind your back. You pushed open the door of the cafe with your foot, chose a table for us in a corner well away from the door and asked the waitress, whose only customers we were, for three pots of hot chocolate with extra whipped cream.

Only now that it was clear we were going to spend the next hour together did I study your face in detail, as best I could in the dim mix of sunlight and lamplight. In spite of the feverish glint in your pupils, which reflected whatever you looked at, your large pale-grey eyes resembled an old carp's. Your soft, unshaven, oval face was pale too, and your left fleshy ear stood out less than the right one did. Strands of your hair, which needed cutting, hung down over your forehead. There were shadows under your eyes, which weren't cast by your long blond lashes or entirely attributable to the diffuse lighting. Your most attractive features were your voluptuous yet virile mouth and your strong, dimpled chin which, when considered in isolation, looked like a stubbly baby's bottom.

The waitress brought three cups, filled them with hot chocolate and replaced the full ashtray with an empty one. Before I could take a first greedy sip, however, you put down next to the rose I'd stuck in a glass of water against the wall the thing you'd kept hidden behind your back and then parked by your chair. 'Open it,' you said, beaming, as Benno sketched a background smile.

I lifted the lid of the slightly damaged purple box and saw, nestling on a bed of wood wool, a breathtakingly disgusting Pierrot, Harlequin or white-faced clown with a conical blue hat, a green ruff, a little button nose, a pouting heart-shaped mouth and a black tear under one of its dumbly staring glass eyes.

For that instant, maybe even for several minutes, I was so stunned that I lost all control of my facial expressions. In any case, that was what I surmised from the ghost of disappointment that flickered across your faces when I was finally capable of looking up, at Benno and then at you. Thank you, I said, my voice almost inaudible.

You didn't reply, but as if he were a master at glossing over tricky situations, Benno began blathering on about how you'd chosen this 'valuable artist's doll, a unique piece of handicraft' over all the other less beautiful ones and had spent 'a pretty penny' on it because you'd reckoned that this, and none other, was the one for me.

This immediately threw me again, but not because I'd started having doubts about *you*. No, I wondered what it was about my appearance that might possibly have prompted you to make a connection or even detect a similarity between this monstrous piece of kitsch and me.

I excused myself, went to the toilets and scrutinized the parts of my person visible above the washbasin: the amateurish pinned-up hairdo that I could no longer even compare to a burst cushion, a bird's nest or an insect's den, my small red mouth and my eyes circled with kohl. You know, I said to the apparition before me, shed a tear now and you can lie down alongside it on that wood wool.

I have no idea, Harry, if any other woman would've come back to you, had she taken her handbag with her and the toilet window not been barred.

Leaving my bag behind, and not with the most trustworthy of strangers either, was not a good sign. Seized by a sudden wave of panic that didn't knock me off my feet for one reason only, namely that since losing my purse I'd kept my money in my bra,

I suppressed the urge that had brought me to this place, along with the barely less urgent one to improve my looks, by dabbing at my eyes with the last brown paper towel peeping out of the dispenser.

Luckily, I found you where you were supposed to be, in the corner at the very back of the cafe, and at least that dispelled my worries about my handbag. You didn't look at me as I plopped down with a sigh onto the empty chair between you, which was not the same one I'd vacated a few minutes earlier. You looked disgruntled, angry in fact. I wondered whether this mood might be due to my lukewarm appreciation of your present and a subsequent argument between the two of you, or whether something else had warped your expressions, some unrelated reason I didn't know about.

I reached for the doll, said in a shrill voice, Pretty—and was shocked by how false this sounded.

'Go on, give it a hug,' Benno insisted, his tone no less fake than mine and extremely patronizing, as if I'd won this horrid doll with a fairground tombola ticket he'd bought me, adding, 'No one can take it away from you now.'

'OK, don't make a meal of it.' That was what you said to put an end to our amateur dramatics, and although you tried to grin, the way you avoided looking at either Benno or me signalled that I'd spoilt the occasion for you. Not only for you; the overall mood had turned sour. We sat there as silent as stones. There was no hot chocolate left either.

Never again could I have made a more easy, a more serene, a more elegant, a smoother exit, and permanently extracted myself from any further dealings with you; I would have needed only to grab my bag, the pitiful rose and the pathetic clown, leave some money between the empty cups and say, That was nice. Only a few steps from the table where the three of us sat amid the wreckage of our meeting was the wide-open door with people strolling past outside, all of them probably feeling better than I did at that one all-important moment when I didn't move my arse and was instead foolish enough to try again to catch your gaze, which had turned very dark, your eyes all pupil and staring for ages into mine.

From that—or was it already from our first?—moment on, I had the creeping feeling that you were more or less what I would've become if fate had decided that I enter the world as a boy in that relatively small part of it that, had it not belonged to the 'hostile political system', I might have called ours or simply Berlin. But as it was, between *your* childhood, puberty and youth and mine there were still—along with ruins, houses, trees, bushes and patches of grass—a wall, anti-tank obstacles and nervous border guards, lusting for medals, bonuses and special leave, who played their part in ensuring that we were separated by more than gender.

My suspicion of being, or desire to be, like you didn't bring us any closer; it was and still is paradoxical, unfathomable, probably only an emotional hallucination. We didn't go together and we didn't suit each other, not in appearance nor in any other way. Instead, it was as if I scented something about you for which I can only think of the lame word 'opposite'. I could say 'contrast', if that didn't carry too strong an inference of something complementary. You were fundamentally different from me then, and probably even more different now. My attempts to fathom you—

always accompanied by misinterpretations, errors and setbacks—might have been purely selfish. Maybe I was hoping, through intimate contact with the stranger you were, or the strangeness with which you acted towards me, that I might be able to fathom myself and simply felt it was less dangerous to discover in you what I only suspected, or might have suspected, in myself. You did things I would never have done but could understand. You were capable of holding back where I opened up, the way I had learnt to—against my will, something I only sensed when you showed me how not to relent, come what may. You did many things I was incapable of; on the other hand, I coped with situations you never got into. And if you were to ask me now—which, thankfully, you never did because I would have lied—I would say no; no, I didn't love you, even though you were like a brother to me (I know of no better word for what I mean) but not a biological brother, rather one with whom I slept, fucked, copulated (which of these terms would you *not* cross out?) whenever I wanted.

The silence was torture; I couldn't hold your gaze any longer, and for at least the next five minutes none of us appeared to have a plan or even a suggestion. Then I did, and it surprised me more than you. Listen, boys, I said as perkily as a gym teacher, I really need to get going, take care of a few things. But if you've got nothing better to do on Sunday, we could all have dinner at my place in Moabit. I'll make asparagus with small schnitzels. Or would you prefer roulade?

Something I was unable to interpret appeared in your face, but then it lit up so brightly, as if all the dark thoughts hiding in the wrinkles above your recently raised eyebrows had crawled forth and mutated, in the space of a second, into glowworms itching to mate. 'Oh yeah!' you exclaimed. 'We haven't had asparagus in ages.'

I wrote down my phone number—my real number—on a serviette, along with my address.

'Ah, Moabit. Nice area too, eh, Ben?' you said cheerfully, dragging out the words weirdly, as if I'd just told a joke you were desperately trying to consign to memory.

We settled on 6 p.m. I put my puppet back in its coffin, wedged the box under one arm, my handbag under the other and the rose between my teeth and, with a wave, got out of there. You'd said you were going to stay on for a bit.

Outside, I took a deep breath and walked aimlessly away. I *did* care whether you'd come—because of you. However, I couldn't have said whether I was more hopeful or more fearful that the day after next I'd be sitting there on my own with my two litres of stock, bowls of fruit salad, four kilos of asparagus and ten schnitzels; those were the quantities I'd need, even if I waited for you in vain and then, not for the first time, put all the food out on the landing for the big family next-door in the middle of the night.

First, behind the Winterfeldtplatz in a pub called The Ape that looked unlikely to tempt you two inside, I treated myself to a beer. I was happy to have escaped the situation and yet I already missed you. I gradually realized that I now knew someone in this city, and a man at that, who wasn't wrapped up in a see-through bag, which I would then have referred to as a cellophane or plastic bag rather than by the stupid name 'carrier bag', which still refuses to trip off my tongue (small sacrifices such as these are, after all, the price of seamless assimilation).

The next morning I had no recollection of the pubs where I had presumably consumed many more drinks, but I did at least remember that I had to be at my flower job at 9.30 on the dot. Strewn between the kitchen and the bedroom I found my bra, knickers, shoes, dress, cardigan and handbag. And also, in the toothbrush glass on the windowsill, well supplied with tap water, your— nonetheless completely wilted—rose.

The only thing that had vanished into thin air, as if I had merely dreamt about it, was the harlequin—along with its crumpled purple cardboard box from which I definitely had not and would not have removed it a second time. Oh Harry, may that box forever preserve our harlequin from harm, wherever he may be—from dogs and cats and the eyes of any creature purportedly endowed with reason.

Food is crap even before it becomes crap and struggles to get back out of us. I've never really liked it, ever since I was a kid. I took what was going, as much as necessary, as little as possible. Turned out it was better that way in the following years. Didn't have to spend money on it, couldn't have spared any either. But now, among the unsuspecting . . . If they're trying to be nice to you, they heap it on your plate. And you've got to shovel it up or they look at you strange. Before I finally put down my fork, I always make a few compliments: great sauce, tastes good, meat's lovely and tender. They beam at you like screwing squirrels.

IV

The stall next to the entrance of the defunct Halensee station was only there at weekends and public holidays in frost-free periods of the year; it belonged to Franz, a quiet, squat bloke of about fifty who, so Christoph said, spoke an eastern Westphalian dialect. In the mornings, when Franz, whose surname I never learnt, hauled the bunches of roses, tulips, chrysanthemums, lilies, gerbera and palm fronds out of his van and in the evenings, when he came to pick up the takings, the more or less empty buckets, the large parasol against the sun and the rain, the two wooden trestles and the heavy door that served as a counter for us—sometimes Christoph, sometimes me—he was always accompanied by Bumblebee, his fat, yellow-and-black-speckled sheepdog bitch, who had a smouldering passion for cold sausages; she seemed not to have any others, though, because she never barked and didn't leave the back of the vehicle until Franz or I had finished setting up the stall and finally ambled over to the kiosk that sold her favourite food, and even then Franz first gave a peculiarly musical whistle to make sure she begged for it properly.

The first time I approached the spot on Halensee bridge Christoph had described, Franz was already unloading bits and bobs onto the road but must have been expecting me and noticed my indecisive interest in his arrangements because he dropped everything, took a few steps towards me and gave me a peculiarly timid nod. He ran his eyes over me quickly from top to bottom before hesitantly offering his hand, which was so rough that I assumed he really was a gardener. Franz looked at my chest because he couldn't return anyone's gaze without going red, and with more indifference than friendliness said: 'You're the new girl. Good. That over there,'—he pointed to a gadget resembling a pair of pliers—'is the thorn stripper you'll need for the roses. The scissors are hanging on the right-hand edge of the board next to a roll of raffia, which belongs with the wrapping paper in the holder in front. There's a set price per stem'—he turned to the buckets— 'but upwards of twenty marks you can give a discount. And these'—he handed me two grubby cigar boxes—'are for the cash. Notes in the smaller one, coins in the bigger one. And this here'— he nudged a stool under the spread parasol with his foot—'is to sit down on when business is slow.'

Franz gave another quick nod, whistled to Bumblebee and a moment later they had disappeared, first into and then with the van.

My first customers were three women who were probably on their way to Charlottenburg for a shopping spree and wanted to kill some time because most of the shops didn't open until ten. They pulled up next to my stall for a minute, got out of their VW and asked for 'fresh stuff, about fifteen marks' worth, nice and colourful, no fern'.

Their impatience grew faster than the mess I was making because they had to watch me repeatedly arranging and rearranging the stems in my clumsy right hand, only ten but still far too many, collapsing into one another over and over again until I managed to bring them more or less under control—and still had only my left hand free to attempt to tie all the wet ends together tightly enough that the bouquet at least somewhat resembled my idea of one. The woman who eventually accepted my effort made no comment; and the next bunch, over which I once more took ages, was grasped and paid for without a word. Only the oldest lady showed me something like condescending, mocking sympathy as I set about composing my third spray. 'Just wrap the whole thing in paper, loose. I'll sort it out myself when I get home,' she said, leaving her change on the counter.

It was quiet for a while after the women had gone. I had time to practise. By noon I was better at it, especially as barely anyone came to buy a flower, let alone a bouquet. But when, from four onwards, men—wreathed in alcoholic fumes—moved in, wanting what Christoph, his eyes gleaming, had called 'dragon fodder' during our 'induction booze-up', the sweat began to gather on my brow again. Although Valentine's Day and Mother's Day had come and gone weeks ago, they queued as they had in the East and exchanged fifty mark notes for fat bunches of long-stemmed Burgundies identical in every way to the rose you gave me soon afterwards, only yours was solo—and remained unique, in both senses of the word.

That Saturday, my third on the stall and the first since we'd met, I asked Franz first thing in the morning if I could knock off early. I invented a divorced sister with three small children who'd suddenly taken ill, so ill that I had to go round and feed the sprogs, wash them, put them to bed and sing them to sleep . . . 'All right,' Franz interrupted me. 'I don't want to know.'

He came back at noon. I wanted to help him load up his stuff, but Franz merely said, 'Leave it, I'm going to carry on selling for a while.'

Not been very busy so far, I'm afraid, I said sheepishly, pushing the cigar boxes towards Franz, but he simply nodded. Not once did I see Franz check or ask how much I'd taken, whether I'd received any tips, maybe bought myself a snack from one of his two tills or given away any flowers. And so I began to steal small sums from Franz, who was paying us eight marks per hour, no less, cash in hand, but I made very sure that the difference between the quantity of missing blooms and the remaining money in the cigar boxes didn't stand out. I had no idea how Christoph dealt with this and didn't dare to find out either because I owed this fantastic job entirely to him. And since I couldn't rule out the possibility that Christoph was honest or at least wasn't cheating to the same extent as I was, I increasingly displaced my petty criminal activities onto the clientele; I didn't round figures down, as Franz had suggested, but systematically charged a few pennies more— for fern, foliage or grasses, which were in fact free or, more accurately, already included in the price of the flowers.

That Saturday before our dinner, I had lied to *and* robbed Franz for the first time because asparagus, even Greek asparagus, was still expensive in mid-April. In addition, I needed beer, wine, cheese, fruit, a tart, chocolate, cognac, scotch, pear brandy . . .

V

Since Sunday morning I'd been as busy as if I were catering for a wedding. The beef consommé, the vanilla pudding with diced apples, oranges and pineapple, and the mixed leaf salad with its separate dressing were standing ready, and the asparagus was on the boil. I'd just begun to coat the nicely tenderized veal escalopes in an eggy gloop of flour and breadcrumbs when the doorbell rang and kept ringing, and not the one downstairs, no, my own front door right behind me. I was so shocked that I stuck my crumb-covered left hand in my hair. Between the bouts of door-bell-ringing I heard whispering; I immediately recognized your voices. You, Harry, laughed—a loud and dirty laugh. Although I felt pretty dirty too, with the breadcrumb mush in my hair and the greasy apron on my sweaty body, I really wasn't up for this. You were early, about two hours early. After making the final preparations for our meal, I'd intended to have a wash, do my hair, put on some makeup, get dressed and set the table. Now, though, all I could do was tear the apron from my waist, pull off my old jeans and put on the same dress again. Hang on, I'm coming, I bleated stupidly, charged back into the kitchen, knocking over two chairs, then, inspired by a spark of intelligence, leapt over them to the shower cubicle, turned on the tap, held my head under the cold water and tried unsuccessfully to fight back my mounting tears. My only consolation was that when I stood before you two or three minutes later with a dripping mane, you wouldn't recognize them as tears.

'Sorry, but we were so bored. Maybe we can help out?' Your left hand held out a wrapped bottle and with the other you made to grab my right hand. But I crossed my arms over my chest and stared at you until you'd wiped off your expressions that suggested everything was hunky-dory.

You kept quiet, but Benno said, 'Hi. We didn't mean to put you out.'

I nodded mutely, gave you cutlery, plates, glasses, a tablecloth and matching serviettes and sent you into the other room. You were soon back, though; Benno leant against the side of the shower cubicle and you perched one buttock on the fridge. Although I'd picked up the two chairs, stacked them and pushed them into the only free corner, it was bloody cramped in the kitchen, even more cramped than usual, and I heard you nattering as I dried my hair over the pan I was frying the meat in.

'Not exactly classy, this place,' you said.

'A shower in the kitchen? Bathtub would be much nicer. We could put it in the middle here and screw a garden hose on the tap over the sink,' Benno said.

'Smells in here,' you said.

'Better to choke than freeze your nads off,' Benno said.

OK, now shut your traps, go in the other room, sit down and open them again; the schnitzels are ready, I said.

As far as I remember, the evening didn't go too badly. The two of you praised more than you ate; I, on the other hand, drank more than you, much more. That food mattered little to you and alcohol not at all, and wine was 'repugnant' to you, like 'sour grape juice'; this and many other things you admitted to me only later.

Some time in the night I must have left my chair, sat down on one of the two mattresses and fallen asleep, just as I was.

When I woke up from thirst or squawking birds or the morning light falling through the windowpanes and looked around, I spotted you on the second mattress; only you—Benno was obviously gone, or at least nowhere near you. Just about avoiding the table covered in the leftovers of our meal and my binge drinking, I staggered out into the hallway, stepped, since I had encountered Benno neither there nor in the kitchen, out of my crumpled dress, which was bizarrely undone down to the last buttonhole, drank some water and searched for my dressing gown, which was not in its usual place on the peg on the back of the door. Wearing a raincoat I'd plucked from the rack in the hall, I tiptoed back to you, saw that you'd used my dressing gown as a blanket, saw your big, narrow feet—and then your face, which was completely relaxed, yes, a picture of relaxation, as if you were lying there fully anaesthetized. Your chin had slumped forward onto your chest; your lips revealed the point of your not-at-all-pointy but actually peculiarly wide tongue, as limp as a dishcloth. And it wasn't only your mouth that was half open but your eyelids too; the eyeballs they barely covered were rolled up or at least so twisted that only the whites were staring out at me. You've been in my life all the time since that Sunday, and your mate Benno never showed up again. When I asked after him once, twice at most, with no particular interest, all you said was, 'No idea where he's got to.'

VI

Late in the morning, I defied a nasty hangover and mustered the energy to do without the next snatch of sleep. I got up off the mattress, threw my covers over you, took a few things out of the wardrobe and went to have a shower, get dressed and prepare breakfast.

I'd just sat down and begun to poke around in some lumpy scrambled eggs with bacon, yawning into my mug, when you appeared in the kitchen doorway, clasping the lapels of my dressing gown over your chest against the cold, lowered yourself onto the seat at the place I'd set for you and, refusing food and coffee, asked only for a drop of Coke.

I felt shit because it had been a long time since I'd had a guest at this time of day and in this state, let alone someone I barely knew but to whom I was anything but indifferent. In attempting to smile in response to what I thought was your dark, critical gaze, I felt how taut the skin over my cheekbones was, how swollen my eyelids still were and that my eyes were weepy. Also, I couldn't shake the thought out of my head that I'd woken up in an unbuttoned dress without any recollection of how it had come to be that way. So had we touched each other, or did I merely wish we had? When I finally managed to return your uncritical but still dark gaze, it was unwavering—and held mine until I was forced to look away.

Do you realize, Harry, how much I admired and hated it, that normal gaze of yours with those dilated pupils, which unintentionally subjugated me, their incomparable calm emptiness giving me full scope for interpretation while ensuring that every attempt at projection simply bounced off you, like a black wave casting me back on myself, something that required strength but also filled me with it.

'So?' you said hoarsely.

I didn't know how to answer that, so I stared for several minutes at a scorch mark on the tabletop, inhaling the smoke from your cigarette through flared nostrils because I didn't want to light one of my own just yet. More out of embarrassment than curiosity, I ended up asking you what your plans were and if we should maybe go for a walk.

'No,' was your reply, 'not today. We could rest a bit more though.'

I wasn't sure what exactly you meant by that. Listening to music in a horizontal position, smoking on your back, falling asleep while watching TV: all of these 'misdemeanours', as you sometimes called them, counted as resting in your book. But I didn't yet know that that Monday and followed you weak-kneed into my room. I sank down onto one of the mattresses, you, to my amazement, not above or at least next to me, but on the other one. We lay completely still, breathing shallowly, almost noiselessly, like lizards in the sun; the only thing I could feel and even hear clearly was the crackle of my hair as our skulls brushed against each other.

I believed you were already asleep and, in my disappointment, had decided to do likewise when you launched into the longest speech you ever made in my presence. You'd only been out of jail, Tegel prison, for a fortnight, on parole because you'd agreed to go to the 'arse-end of the city', Düppel-Süd, to take part in some kind of 'therapy-instead-of-punishment scheme under paragraph 35 of the Narcotics Act'. Soon, though, there'd been 'an incident, nothing serious, just a small breach of the farmyard rules' but you'd been threatened with the 'most terrible consequences'. As a result, you had 'hammered into' your friend Benno, who'd been sentenced with you for 'aggravated robbery', that you needed to 'show these nitpickers a big fat finger' and 'break out, first of all'.

You said this slowly, quietly and lying down. I, though, had shot up from my mattress at the word 'jail' and loomed over you in the classic position—legs wide, clenched fists resting on my hips; but you just pulled a mocking face as if you could see me with your eyes closed. Your hand crawled out from under the covers like a spider, groped for one of my bare feet, clasped my ankle—as if it were an insect—and pressed with such surprising force that I knelt down in front of you. You put an arm around my neck, and I nestled my face against your chest. Though more excited than aroused, I was expecting more and, despite the tight hold you had on me, tried to accommodate, even anticipate you by tearing at the buttons of my fly.

The ruse, or whatever it was, by which you released all the air from me like an inflatable animal consisted of giving me a small and almost ridiculously gentle peck, a child's kiss, causing my cheek to burn for hours as if something had stung or bitten me.

I hadn't imagined that *I* might receive *that* kind of kiss, not then, not this many years too late, never in fact. And the word 'child's kiss' isn't quite accurate because your first kiss, Harry, wasn't *from* a child but *for* a child, and had it not been so incredibly tender and I so nonplussed, I would have thought: He doesn't want me— or he only wants to take the piss out of me. Since that second when your lips dodged mine, touching only the left corner of my mouth and me even more deeply, I knew: this is the kiss no one gave me at an age when kisses like that ought to have been normal.

I can only compare my shock at this, the subsequent mixture of sorrow and a little joy, with the feeling that took hold of me when I flew from Ulaanbaatar to Irkutsk in May 1984, two years before moving to *your* Germany, and, spotting the forest alongside the runway, stood and laughed through my tears because the sight of those Siberian spruces reminded me that I hadn't seen a single tree for ten months. Do you understand? It was only when I saw trees again that I realized I'd missed them and how badly.

Your kiss provoked a similarly sweet pain, especially as the burning that followed must have been purely down to shame; I suddenly realized something else: all the kisses I could remember, even the earliest ones, were what I'd been expecting from you and not received, and vice versa. Harry, you gave your unsettlingly innocent, brutally tender debut kiss to someone for whom self-pity was relatively new, someone who, prior to that lingering second when she received that non-sexual kiss, would not have believed it possible that she might have longed for precisely such a kiss as a child—and never for one of the other kisses. And now I'm telling you what you weren't to know at the time because I would only have been ashamed and might perhaps have embarrassed you: even the fatherly kisses little Soya had once tolerated, gagging on them like lumpy rice pudding, were men's kisses, and clumsy ones at that, which she hadn't enjoyed but had thought inescapable.

And the men who alternated with and eventually replaced my father kissed no differently and no better. And there had been no motherly or grandmotherly kisses; and later, when a few women did kiss me, there was not much to choose between their kisses and the men's and, all in all, not much to make me prefer them.

'Anyway, Soya,' you said as I lay clinging to your chest, rising and falling passively with it, 'the thing is, I'm in a fix: there's an arrest warrant out for me because I've violated the terms of my parole by escaping and defying the therapy the courts ordered. And if I don't start therapy with a different accredited place soon, I'll be back in the pen.'

I didn't really catch the full gist of your speech, partly because I was too absorbed with myself or, more accurately, with the turmoil into which your kiss had plunged me, and asked: What do you mean, 'pen'? Therapy for what?

Then you pronounced that strangely melodious word that only added to my confusion, even though, or precisely because, I didn't understand English but somehow knew that the context in which I'd heard or read it before was desperately grim: 'junkie'. From you, for the first time, I learnt what it meant—not 'drug addict', as the dictionary states, but (human) trash, rubbish, refuse, garbage.

Fear was never my reason for trying to kick the habit. When you're in the clink, it doesn't matter if you carry on or if you kick the bucket first. One's no more appealing than the other. When things are normal you've always got something to do and you spend your time getting hold of money, stashing dope, tending to your veins, the anticipation and the disappointment because the junk doesn't feel as good as it used to or it's so tainted it just makes you sick. But you don't want to croak, like a fly that refuses to be swatted: it may not have a brain, but it's alive anyway. Resolutions are for when you get out and for New Year's Day. As getting out comes closer, even Easter or Whitsun is like New Year's Day.

I don't know why I could barely react, whether it was down to the kiss, to the fact that he hadn't sent me recoiling into the barbarism of my childhood and yet had weirdly awoken a desire inside me to be small again and be kissed that way many more times. Or was it your half-closed eyelids that moved me, and the shadows under them? Or did I feel something like relieved pity because despite being nicked over 'on the other side' for more or less serious troublemaking, unlike you, maternal influence had helped *me* escape actual prison and not just the one named East Germany?

In any case, I maintained a dogged and convincing silence for a while. Maybe that was why you had to go on talking, telling me about yourself, about your father, a haulier in Neukölln who allegedly pushed your mother out of the window of your flat when you were four. She may also have fallen either deliberately or by accident because she'd drunk more than a little, always had, as your father said; to ease the pain, you thought. You'd been sent to live with your grandmother in Lüneburg and stayed there until her second husband suddenly died. You had to go to school anyway, so your father took you back and left you to his new wife, whose name was Rosi. Your father had called her Rosinante though—and so had everyone else. 'This Rosi, known as Rosinante but whose real name might be Roswitha, isn't one of us, she's a brawny Palatine.'

I pondered this description; 'brawny' and 'Palatine' sounded stranger to me than words like 'fragile' and 'Surinam'. The Palatine was somewhere in Germany. But how was I to imagine 'brawny'?

'You know, coarse,' you answered, 'Rosinante was coarse, ordinary, a pot on little skinny legs, like Don Quixote's old mare. Why do you think we found Rosi less fitting than Rosinante and, occasionally, Auntie Rosinante?'

Rosinante ran a pub, a 'horrible, stale-aired dive', 'obviously and inappropriately' named The Rose. 'And hanging on to her apron strings,' you said, 'was a kid my age, Fat Bernie.' He was 'in a pretty bad way' and grizzled a lot 'for no reason and, more often than not, for a good one.'

This Bernie and you grew up with Rosinante behind the bar of The Rose. Every afternoon you would carry your plastic Indians and your Lego blocks in there, along with your torches of course, because without them it would have been too dark to play. Otherwise, you mostly 'kept quiet'—firstly because you weren't supposed to annoy the guests, and secondly because the two of you had almost nothing to say to each other anyway. Bernie, that 'great wimpy malco', really couldn't 'keep up with you', but it wasn't as if you 'didn't care less about him'. He was a failure at school long before you were and he also 'rolled the first joints' when you were just about tall enough to peek over the counter, big enough in any case to wash glasses or pull pints and fetch your own food from the pub kitchen, always the same things: sausages, frankfurters, meatballs, gherkins and ice-cold potato salad. No one took proper care of you. The guests were either sullen or tanked or both; Rosinante was always serving, unloading, clinking glasses, falling over or dozing off, your father either on the road or 'flying off the handle' on the few occasions he showed up to see his 'patched-up family'.

Then one Sunday in August—Bernie had just turned twelve and you were about to—the old man had 'given you such a shoeing' that you decided to kill yourselves with meatballs; more precisely, you would poison the meatballs and then 'the two of us would poison ourselves with them'. You got four packets of HB from the cigarette machine, removed the filters, peeled the tobacco out of the paper and mixed it into the mince, which was seasoned, bulked up with shredded white bread and ready to fry. 'Rosinante didn't notice a thing when she lit the stove, divvied up the mixture and tossed the flattened lumps into the hot oil. They smelt the same and tasted as bad as ever, we thought, one hour and many meatballs later. Bernie went green in the face first and didn't even make it to his feet to puke, let alone to the toilet.' You followed his lead not long afterwards and, you stressed, 'with far more dignity'. You were taken to the hospital to have your stomachs pumped and were ill for several days, as were five of Rosinante's regulars, despite eating only one or two of the tobacco balls. It all came out: first out of you, 'top and bottom', and then your plan too, following an analysis of the stomach contents of everyone affected.

Your father beat you both again, but only when he was no longer worried about dirtying his hands 'on your stupid little arses'.

A whole week after the 'last thrashing I ever stood for', the 'old dung beetle' casually announced that your mother's mother, your beloved Lüneburger grandma, had 'bitten the dust'—'literally' because she'd succumbed to a heart attack while 'cutting grass for the rabbits' behind her house, ironically on the same day as your failed suicide attempt.

Here you fell silent, and I was still lying on your warm, woolly chest. And as I pictured you rolling around behind the bar of The Rose, puking and writhing with stomach cramps, you fell asleep. I felt tired too; and the images of you as a boy and a callow, spotty youth called Bernie I didn't know and was never to meet were replaced by other ones:

I'm about half a year older than you were in your meatball stage and I'm with my little sister, my mother and my father at the secluded lake in the woods near our summerhouse in Brandenburg. My parents and I are cheerful, a rare occurrence; only my hydrophobic sister Olga, who owes her name to my mother's second idol, the German communist Olga Benário, murdered in the Bernburg Euthanasia Centre in 1942, is sitting sourly a little distance from us at the foot of a weeping willow that leans out over the lake because she knows the rest of us are soon going to go swimming and will—unsuccessfully as always—urge her to come in with us.

My mother, six feet tall and solidly built, is the first to get undressed and climbs naked 'up the willow', as she announced solemnly. I go to the edge of the lake and study her closely, almost fixedly, with irritation but without pity; her flabby, stretch-marked tummy and her heavy breasts with their brown nipples which are obscenely stiff despite the warm air but pointing downwards as they rest on the two white fleshy pads—like barnacles, I think, and then: like warts. My mother ducks her head with its peroxide curls between her outstretched arms, flexes at the knees and jumps. There's an explosion and water splashes back in the direction from which my mother—invisible for a few seconds—came. She reappears well to the left of the whirlpool she has created and gives the kind of muffled growl my old teddy makes when I tilt it over backwards. My mother lets out a roar of laughter, immediately raising one of her arms from the surface; the hand on the end of it waves to me. 'Your turn, Soyushka! Don't chicken out. Climb up into the top branches. Show me what you can do, Soyush. I want to see you dive. No more cannonballs.' And I gather my courage and stretch my arms above my head just as I've seen my mother do so many times and plunge down. And I do manage to dive fairly straight into the water, which is green and full of bubbles which carry me back up to the surface, rejoicing that for once I might actually have made my mother happy. And she is indeed grinning from ear to ear as she swims towards me and says, 'Climb on my back, my brave little girl,' because she knows there's nothing I like more than that. And I put my arms around her waist, and my smooth, flat, girly stomach briefly touches her cold bottom. My mother fools around like a hippo; she splutters and snorts and drags me through the water, and I catch hold of one of her churning legs and fail to notice my father creeping up behind us. Only when he suddenly reaches out and squeezes my small breasts like half lemons do I realize it must be him. I scream in shock and pain, let go of my mother and thrash around in terror. My father's hands release me—and I cannot breathe. My vision goes black, my ears are filled with a rushing and a roaring, my arms and legs are out of control and soon I can't move them; I sink down and down to the bottom of my very first blackout.

I might have told you that story back then if you hadn't been so fast asleep and if my eyes hadn't closed too, from despair that my stupid mother never noticed anything and that I could never tell her in all those years, and also from happiness, happiness at being with you and nowhere else.

I woke up because your hand was working its way under my waistband and stroking my stomach, not forcefully or expectantly, not like a tailor's hand checking if the new fabric is fine enough, nor like a hand massaging a baby with indigestion, but not far off. And we ended up doing it, neither casually nor enthusiastically but as part of the whole thing because we wanted to be part of each other's lives. That first time, and again and again in subsequent intimate moments, you treated me—and I mean this in the medical sense of the word—you treated me as if you needed to soothe and appease me, even though I'd never been on edge or wild. I knew I could come fast and rely on your cock which, true to the cliché, was like your hands: strong, warm and not too sensitive.

You lay there under me, utterly submissive, neither moaning nor opening your eyes to look into mine, but when you noticed I was done, you pulled out of me, took me by the hips and 'fetched me down from the pole', as you called it. I wondered if you'd forgotten during your ten years in prison that women took the pill and asked if it had been OK for you.

'You can carry on if you like,' you said. But when you realized how I'd interpreted this, you grabbed my hair with one hand and held me away from your cock and pulled one of my hands, the wrong one unfortunately, towards where you didn't want my mouth. I accepted this, but it did set me thinking—and once more I asked myself, not you, whether maybe you were scared I might bite you or just not be up to it, although my oral skills were the only ones I was genuinely proud of. Whatever, I'll bring you round, I thought as I finished off what you had, after all, allowed— and there I was wrong again.

As I soon noticed, sex was the most normal thing in the world for you, but not the most important. I liked sex too, as you know, but only if I wasn't in love or not very much. My favourite thing— and probably most other people's—or in fact the only thing I liked about it, were orgasms, explosions so powerful they blew all my fuses and disconnected my mind from the grid for a moment. I owe the greatest highs of my life to those moments; even the wildest drinking binge couldn't produce such a total absence from myself, everyone and everything else. The craters swallowed me up and then spat me back out, intact, I thought, and I focused on directing the action from their edges. I found it more interesting to manipulate the other person than to be touched myself. Nothing else gave me such a sense of power and importance. Yes, Harry, I aspired to be a good lover, if only to offset my physical shortcomings. My experience, both before and after you, was that many women, and every single one of the not frightfully large number of men who sought to get close to me, wanted to take me to bed. Some out of athletic ambition, others as collectors; I had no idea what else they might have wanted from me. The men in particular tended to recognize instantly that sex was enough, and that something as complicated as love would only irk me. When I did fall in love, I suffered from a variety of complexes and felt ugly, stupid and ill. And there was only one remedy for the love disease I feared more than death: sex—with a nice person as different as possible from the creature I idolized. And yet, Harry, whenever I noticed that I was going down with love again, I longed to reach an age when I genuinely believed I'd need no further antidote and would no longer be obsessed with power, because my sexuality would have at last become completely irrelevant—both to others and to myself.

The plan to get my own pad is off until further notice. My motto now is stay out for as long as possible. I can imagine anything: 'no more rainbows', breaking my back down the pit, losing both hands tomorrow or croaking the day after, just not being locked up again for my whole stretch. If I'm reading the signs properly and I can put steps in place on Monday, that'll avert the danger for now and life will be almost sweet.

VII

On Monday morning, only my dressing gown, a pillow and the covers were lying on the mattress you'd claimed as your own, but on the kitchen shelf by the stove were three fresh rolls, my pile of money with a tenner missing and a note: 'Dear Soya, just got to clear something up quickly. Back soon, with the cash. So long, Harry.'

I didn't have the slightest doubt that you'd be back, strangely, but your highhandedness annoyed me. You could have whispered in my ear or at least given me a kiss. After my first roll with jam, however, I figured that you'd chosen not to wake me out of simple kindness. I wasn't floating on cloud nine on account of the hours I'd spent with you, I wasn't even happy; at most I was surprised about how quickly everything was moving and that I was no longer alone. I could see you before me, a fully grown West Berliner: tall, athletically built, a broad forehead whose paleness was striking without being posh, a dimple in your chin, blue-grey eyes capable of a magnificent scowl; and I had a shot of pear brandy to celebrate my conquest, because that, Harry, is how I still thought of you that morning. The fact that you'd been in prison—and for quite a long stretch—only enhanced your nobility. Where I came from it was easy to pick up ten years for a trifle such as cracking a joke, forging a cheque or stealing public property. Reflecting on the last of these offences, I was reminded of your casual mention of 'aggravated robbery' and decided to ask you straight out what that meant.

The aggravated robbery, you explained two hours later, was a 'pharmacy break-in', and one of the police officers who had 'interrupted' you had 'stupidly' been shot, but not by you. You'd 'just been a lookout, as always, during a botched attempt to bag some opiates'. The sentence had 'been set unreasonably high' because you were considered a 'repeat offender' and were 'still on parole'. 'But now,'—you took a long drag on your cigarette—'we need to forget about these rancid stories and focus on what comes next.' There was this thing in Schöneberg, in Eisenacher Strasse, a 'tough bunch' called the Triad, 'like the Chinese mafia', you added with a grin. You'd already had a quick word with the 'crew's boss man' to explain your situation and he'd said the 'matter wasn't completely hopeless'. 'He wants us to come today, you and me. Please, dollymouse, my fate's in your hands,' you said, and you were clever enough to hug me to your chest again and give me a solemn and timid kiss on the forehead.

So, without asking or saying anything, I did up my hair in a smart ponytail, put on my Helmut Kohl cardigan, slipped my ID card into my pocket and walked to the subway station with you.

The house, whose carved double wooden doors, flanked by genuine or fake marble pillars, you held open for me, was one of those Wilhelmine blocks, more correctly known as buildings, which people like us don't usually enter without good reason or without some trepidation. Inside, it smelt slightly of disinfectant and paper and therefore of hospitals and government offices. The wide, long corridors—typical of both—were painted white; there was a board with directions, a few pictograms, and plaques with names and numbers on them above, below and alongside various lamps, switches and bells.

At the end of the eastern corridor on the ground floor you knocked on the last door on the left, the only one with no writing or number on it. Though there was no doorbell either, there was a buzzing noise; I heard firm, quick steps and saw the handle on our side of the door go down and then, indistinctly at first against the bright neon strip lighting, a rather small, compact man of about thirty.

'Ah, come in,' he said without offering you or me his hand. As the door closed behind us, I noticed out of the corner of my eye the Che Guevara poster stuck to the back of it. The man continued talking as we made our way to the four folding chairs arranged along the near side of one of three desks. 'I'm Joe, plain Joe, as Harry knows already. And you are?'

Soya Edith Krüger. I live in Moabit, Birkenstrasse 11, I replied, sounding like a warped vinyl record. I didn't appreciate the sergeant-major-like tone in which this Joe had just spoken to me, and I wanted him to know it.

'Krüger?' you repeated and took this opportunity to remark that we had the same surname. —That's right, Harry: 'had', because my name has been Maiwald since my subsequent, short marriage to a semi-gay Swiss man you never met.

'Soya should do just fine,' Joe said before proceeding to explain that the two of us, you and I, had to set up a so-called 'support group' before the end of the week. The first stage of the Triad would require at least eight, if possible ten or twelve, 'reliable people who are clean, meaning not addicted to any hard drugs' who would 'take turns' putting you up for the night, 'feeding him, keeping him busy, bringing him to therapy and picking him up again, on the absolute dot'. 'Keep an eye on time, live by the clock' was the main lesson an addict needed to learn. 'If you or any of your support groupies is even a few minutes late, you'll be out and I hope you, Harry, are damn well aware of what the consequences would be.' The second stage was on the same level as the first and consisted of face-to-face meetings with the aim of 'working through multitoxic experiences', exploring your 'psychological profile' and 'raising your conflict threshold'. He or one of his colleagues would hold these regular conversations with you two or three times a week throughout the 'collective phase' and for longer 'if there was a need on your part'; that would depend on the progress you made. The third stage of the Triad was the 'step towards complete independence, meaning looking for a flat and a job, administrative stuff'. Four further 'unannounced tests for opiates' would be spaced out over these last months, and then you'd be done. Joe didn't take his eyes off you as he spoke, then, after a pause for breath of which neither you nor I took advantage to ask a question, he clapped his hands and said, 'OK, Harry, come with me. You wait here, Soya.'

I sat there alone on my folding chair and wondered whether Joe was Joe's real name and where he might have taken you and what he might want from you there and why he derided the *controlletti* foreseen in his plan as 'support groupies' and what a stupid expression 'damn well aware' was, particularly coming from the big, thin-lipped gob of a pseudo-authoritarian greenback who wanted people to call him, of all things, Joe.

I stood up, but instead of going out for a smoke I walked around the room, which had obviously only very recently been furnished and occupied. There were no plants, no books on the shelves, not even a mug or a soft toy, no pictures other than the one of the *Comandante*, neither on the Formica desktop nor on the freshly whitewashed woodchip wallpaper, just a giant month-by-month calendar bearing the discreet logo of a West Berlin pharmaceutical company whose current page someone, presumably Joe, had filled in with red, blue and green numbers, letters, dots and lines in small, neat handwriting. I studied these symbols for a while but couldn't make head nor tail of the pedantic chaos.

When the two of you returned, you, Harry, had red blotches on your pale, glistening face, however, you looked fairly relieved. Joe's expression was also less deliberately fierce, his gaze duller or perhaps somewhat disappointed or maybe just tired. Stretching his hands out towards us, the right one to you, the left to me, Joe said, 'Make sure you've sorted it by 7 p.m. Friday. I want the whole group here. It's not impossible that some of them might have jobs, hence the late timing. Your lead, Soya. We probably can't rely on Harry's dodgy acquaintances. And tell them there's a one-mark allowance for every hour they give Harry, plus travel expenses and a fixed sum for food, washing powder and stamps. That should help them decide.'

Joe let go of me but not of you—and strangely contorted, he stood facing you like a comedian doing a little-man-peering-through-a-telescope sketch, trying to look you in the eye even though you were staring at your feet.

'Come back at eleven tomorrow for a urine test and every day after that until I say otherwise. If that doesn't pan out, the rest is screwed and I'll call your parole officer.'

With these final words, Joe ushered us towards the door with his arms at right angles to his body and his fingers spread; standing in the doorway, silhouetted against the reflections of the bright, flickering neon light, he cut the figure of a criminal who's just been arrested—or a traffic policeman at dusk on a Berlin crossroads.

As we walked down Eisenacher Strasse towards the subway station, you put your arm around my shoulders and your hand down my cleavage. Your warm breath made the hairs on the back of my neck stand up.

'So, Soya,' you whispered in my ear, 'fancy another hot chocolate?'

I shook my head but you pulled me towards the nearest cafe; and once we'd stepped through the door, suddenly you didn't want hot chocolate any more but 'a double Baileys with a tonne of ice'. You ordered me a pint of wheat beer without asking.

On Monday night I couldn't sleep, and not only because you showed no interest in sleeping with me. The second you lay down on your mattress you shut down for conversation. For a while I tried to peer into your eyes through the occasionally fluttering lids, which were for once fully closed, and fetch you back from the dream that was furrowing your brow. Then, however, I got up from the edge of the mattress and, trying to avoid making any noise, searched for my phone book, a pad and a pencil. I added a bottle of wine and a glass to the ashtray on the kitchen table to help me think better.

Who was I going to invite aboard? I didn't know many people here yet. And why would any of them understand that I needed them because I needed you, a junkie, albeit one who was apparently clean or had at least passed today's urine test? This business would be time-consuming, and the punctuality rule would scare off these free spirits, layabouts like us.

Going through my phone book, I jotted down about fifteen names and numbers on the top sheet of the pad and told myself that eight would be enough. What, though, if the ones I hoped to persuade didn't stick it out or if they suddenly remembered they had to travel somewhere and threw in the towel long before the two months were up? It occurred to me that I could ask Joe—or was it better not to?—and I also remembered the money he'd mentioned. After all, none of the twenty or so eligible people, meaning adults on this side of the wall whose contacts I had, was sufficiently well-off not to jump at the chance of a little extra cash. Also, I already had two of the minimum of eight I needed: myself and, most likely, Christoph. Christoph, who wasn't keen on every woman, as I knew from personal experience, but was keen on many other things, would be glad to be out of the running now that I'd found you and would not refuse me this little favour. I could try blackmailing him, if necessary, by ending our partnership at the flower stall, which would however only worsen and deepen my—I mean, our—problems. After all, if you hadn't been completely skint you wouldn't have borrowed a tenner without saying anything on the morning of only our second day together, and I wouldn't have paid for your earlier Baileys or my beer out of my own pocket. I'll have to talk to you later, as carefully as possible, as clearly as necessary, when you wake up, about how this is going to work financially, I thought and thought and thought, staring into my once-more-empty glass, almost blind with tiredness.

It was getting light as I raised my head from the kitchen table, put the three empty wine bottles in the bin, washed my face and took the butter out of the fridge and the bread out of its bag. I drained a glass of tap water, made some coffee, which I poured into a thermos, spread jam on a slice of bread and wolfed it down in a couple of bites, dressed, stuffed my diminished funds into my bra and looked in on you one more time.

The morning sun was slanting in through the dirty window-panes onto your damp, shiny forehead. I lifted the covers under-neath which, I was touched to see, you were again wearing my dressing gown, ran my fingers over your hair, your eyebrows, your lips; you didn't feel anything. I knew that if I lay down now I would sleep until midday, but in a few hours' time I needed to call the candidates for our group. What was I supposed to do until then other than go for a little walk outside?

I'd almost reached the bottom of the stairs when a vague premonition I'd prefer not to call distrust made me turn around and take along the two hundred-mark notes I kept behind the shower cubicle for emergencies.

It was ages since I'd been out on the streets of Moabit so early in the morning and rarely—in fact never—had I seen them so empty. Few cars broke the unfamiliar silence; only the swifts high up in the cloudless sky were calling as they chased insects or one another. A man stuck his drunken mug out of the wide-open window of a bar that never closed on the corner of Waldstrasse and Turmstrasse, blinked confusedly, retreated, drew the curtain and was cut off from the outside world. A flock of sparrows swarmed a pink hawthorn in bloom; the birds alighted on the branches and began to squabble, their screeching more anxious than loud, as if they realized they were doing the wrong thing but didn't know what the right thing might be. The broken glass piled high on the deck of a barge moored in the Westhafen port twinkled with such alluring malice that I could neither look at it more closely nor fully avert my gaze.

I sat down on the wall of the quay, lit the next cigarette from the butt of its predecessor and stared out over the waters of the Spree. Since you had turned up, I'd been more taken with activism than by you, but what might have blossomed into meaningful activity, I thought, was now dulled by the sun's warmth. Was it perhaps that I had been assigned, even gifted a task that finally gave me another chance not to fight *against* something, as I had always done, but *for* someone who needed me and whose 'fate', he had said, albeit with a laugh, was now 'in my hands'?! In my mind's eye I saw your sleeping face, so pale, so trusting that I ventured to hope that the next few weeks and months would be magical, a breeze—a ten-strong team with the strength of a hydra, requiring only six more heads to add to yours, mine, Christoph's and Joe's.

Shortly after eight o'clock I bought a carton of chocolate drink and half a raw-mince sandwich at the counter of the Westhafen canteen and very slowly continued the stroll that my life might resemble from now on.

At ten o'clock, I was back at Turmstrasse subway station. And since I was afraid that, apart from Christoph, virtually none of the people I wanted to win over for our cause would be up before eleven, I bought a purse at Karstadt that was as cheap as the one I'd lost and looked exactly the same, along with a fairly expensive red dressing gown because I'd decided to let you keep mine; I'd need one too, at least off and on.

Got to see it through, no matter how. It'll be all the better afterwards. I can't afford more than two or three Diazepam a night until Triad Joe stops leering at his charges' dicks while they're pissing. But why would he? Must be hard to fool the guy with a fake urine test. He knows all the tricks; he isn't a social worker. And running off to Spain or somewhere, no way, not enough dosh. No one's going to believe a bloody word I say with these doe eyes of mine.

Again, you weren't at home. I knew, though, that you had to see Joe at eleven on the dot and the earliest you could be back was in an hour, so I sat down and placed the phone on my lap. I usually dealt with the hardest thing first, but this time the easiest was hard enough. I was embarrassed to ask people I hardly knew for help, revealing to them that I was desperate to hold on to yet another person I hardly knew, which meant that I was beholden to them.

I phoned Christoph first, even though I suspected he'd already be gone, but he picked up after the second ring.

'It's you. That's good, I was about to call,' he said cheerfully, telling me before I could get a word in that he was ill, 'with a sick note', because he couldn't stand university any longer and wanted to go to London for the weekend with Bruce. Could I take on another 'flower shift', meaning stand in for him next Saturday? he asked.

Spotting my chance, I plunged into his stream of words: Sure, I will, but only if you're willing to give me, or rather us, a hand with something incredibly important. This opening gambit caught Christoph's attention, and I even managed to spit out a few coherent sentences about you, me and Triad Joe. Please, Christoph, I said, you only need to turn up to this initial group meeting, after that you can be ill or elsewhere for all I care. I'll fill in for you at the stall and with Harry too, whenever you want, whenever you've got something better to do or don't have time to work. I'll also gladly give up a third of the cash that would actually be yours and only goes to me because every so often you can't make it. Maybe I can even persuade Franz to fork out a bit more; after all, I'm pretty good at flogging his foliage and, what's more, it'll be peak season soon. And just so you know, there's cash for Harry as well; you'll get that and you can have mine too, whether you look after Harry or I take your shift.

'Well,' Christoph said, 'since you and this Harry guy seem to be inseparable, I'll be doing you a favour by not bottlefeeding your sweet little toadstool very often. I do want to have a good look at him, though.'

I was furious with myself because I'd gone a bit too far and, instead of attempting to blackmail Christoph, had actually offered him generous bribes for no reason, though now there was at least a chance he wouldn't turn me down. And indeed Christoph said that seeing this meant so much to me, he'd 'go along with this probably pointless altruistic experiment just this once'; he also found 'the idea of a one-third share' of my flower-selling income 'thoroughly acceptable'.

Switched pavement, pretended not to recognize him but clearly saw that T. saw me. He'll let the cat out. Thing is, where are they going to look for me? The only one who knows is my old mate B. Still, need to brief him somehow, but I'll have to find him first and he seems to have vanished off the face of the earth these last couple of days.

Christoph's deliberately nasal and clichéd farewell 'Ciao, bella' was still ringing in my ears and I was wondering how to proceed, alphabetically or by gut instinct, when you appeared silently behind me and touched the back of my neck. I started because I didn't remember straight away that I'd put my spare key beside your mattress. You tossed me a flowery green plastic hairslide, took it back again, grabbed one of the curls of my fringe in your other hand, clipped it in place with a hairdresser's deft touch, kissed me on the head and told me it looked really pretty.

You were gone a long time, I said.

'Dug through the whole shop for that thing,' you said placidly, as if you hadn't noticed the reproachful tone in my voice. Your fingers stroked the slide and my head, which grew emptier and heavier and sank towards your tummy. I no longer felt like thinking about the people I still had to call, only of undoing your shirt, pushing my tongue into your belly button and you to the floor, but an irreducible residue of responsibility resisted, negating the horny combination of ignorance, arrogance and desire that was threatening to get the better of me or even us.

Don't *you* know someone who could join our team, I asked.

Refusing to meet my eyes, yours softened and became blurred as if you were about to cry. You said 'Maybe' in a similar tone of voice, pulled a brown imitation-leather case from the back pocket of your jeans and took from it two slightly faded colour photos; one of a black horse and its young and very pretty rider, the other of the same girl sitting in the corner of a sofa on her own. A sleeveless light-blue T-shirt hugged the half-globes of her pert breasts, which were unconstrained by a bra and between which a long string of pearls was dangling. Her thick blond hair was parted in the middle and hung down to her shoulders; her naturally red lips were slightly open and her eyes looked down in concentration through thick eyelashes at a cigarette she was rolling with obvious style.

'That's Maria,' you said. 'She's as clean as a water droplet, but she just stopped writing back one day.' And you told me more about this Maria, the 'daughter of a true Christian couple', who 'lives in a village near Münster' and 'has a soft spot for long-term

inmates', what a gentle soul she was and how touchingly unsoph-
isticated her last letter, written on yellow paper, had been. She had
also visited you three times in prison, read out Bible passages to
you, held your hand, looked at you with her 'huge blue saucer-
like eyes', it had never occurred to you to 'come on to her' or to
'misuse' one of the colour photos you'd specifically requested as 'a
wanking aid'.

Münster, I said curtly, isn't that a bit far away? I had trouble
hiding the fact that I was jealous—and envious, most of all envious.
I'm not generally inclined to jealousy, even less so now I'm older.
Yet if that undignified feeling took hold of me, an expression of
mean-spirited possessiveness, nothing more, then it generally consisted of envy at the charms of another, more beautiful person. As
for this epitome of rustic innocence, whose name was, for good
measure, Maria, it was your hypocritical ravings about her sup-
posedly so precious purity that pained me most. Yesterday, you let
me fuck you but not give you a blowjob, and today?! While I was
busy saving your skin, regardless of the consequences, you were
confessing your love for a possibly underaged, skinny, straw-blonde
horse freak who couldn't even afford proper cigarettes, satisfying
her—incidentally, totally un-Maria-like—smoking habit with
baccy from a bag, probably because her meagre allowance wouldn't
cover oats, curry comb, fake pearls and yellow flowery letter paper
otherwise.

No, Harry, I didn't ask any more questions or for Maria's
number and address. You must at least have realized that I didn't
want to meet her, meaning that I didn't want her in the group but
to stay forever in the church of her village that was thankfully at

least eight hours away by train, or else roaming the deepest, darkest woods on her bloody nag, for without another word you stuffed the two pictures back in your back pocket, never to appear again.

You stood by the table for a while, silently enduring my sulky silence, before muttering 'I'm tired' and moving into the kitchen, taking your covers and mattress with you. It didn't look as if you were keen for me to follow you.

My depressed mood following the Maria episode resulted in my conducting the next phone calls in a not excessively imploring tone of voice, and this in turn resulted—three hours and seventeen calls later—in my having not only the requisite eight men and women but a backup too.

Flushed with pride, I rushed into the kitchen, drew myself up with crossed arms in front of your resting, maybe even sleeping figure and said very loudly: Hey, Harry, done deal. I've snared our nine guardian angels. —It had been like that from the start, so I wonder if you could even have noticed, but I felt slightly alienated every time I heard myself speaking to you, because the words I used, anticipating that they would be to your taste, were always different from the ones I'd had in mind just a second earlier. I was practising a role that I liked but didn't suit me; I'd love to know— and not merely out of vanity—if you saw through this act but enjoyed my duplicity regardless.

VIII

I've attracted a couple of sweet fools, I really have. The funniest is Clara, an ultra-left-wing pushover who stinks of slutty perfume, writes love poems and claims she used to dance in the ballet. She's bound to have a thing for a cute ex-con like me. I'll call her Clarita and wrap her around my little finger. Nor should Marlene, the Black Forest cougar, cause me too much trouble. Looks like a poodle that's drunk vinegar, but she sings in a band and loves The Doors. Says she's got all their records. Good times ahoy! Then there's Julia, who was probably parched, flat as a pancake and an all-round bore even before puberty, gazing around sadly with those green soft-toy eyes and saying she'd rather people called her Juli because she's just broken up with a Romeo. Although she's a trained goldsmith, Juli works nights manning the hotline for Grieneisen funeral parlour. She's spent the past three summers selling handmade fashion jewellery in Formentera. She's going to skip that this year, though, partly for my sake and partly because she always had to shell out the dosh she'd earnt on a hotel, beach lounger and sangria. One guy's called Frank, a painter from the East, a bearded old codger who thought I might spend my time with him posing as a model. No probs, I said, portrait or nude? His wife Hanna, who's also in our club, has legs up to her neck, mitts like a mason and Klaus Kinski's mouth, and is in the same line of business as him. All she wanted to know is if I can wash up, clean and iron. I'll do the lot once and so badly she never asks me to do any of that shit ever again. Thomas, a blond guy from the Lower Rhine, and his mate Christoph, a podgy Bavarian who wears leather jeans, think they're real high fliers. But how are they going to get high? No idea what their big plan is. Contacts? Tips about how to get some? A few karate lessons from Grizzlyman Harry? The backup is Marc, an American sculptor who is calmness personified and the only one of the bunch I respect.

Of me, Harry, not a single word, not even here in this comparatively detailed passage of your logbook—or whatever you call it. Why am I missing, as if we'd never met? One suspicion I have, the more charitable one, is that you were worried your notebook might fall into the wrong hands during a house search, a fresh arrest, a surprise visit from old acquaintances . . . and so to prepare for that eventuality, you felt it necessary to rule out any textual interpretation that might possibly point in my direction by erasing me altogether. My other supposition, which credits you with less noble motives and is obviously more painful for me, despite being totally compatible with the first, is that you were as indifferent to me as you were to everything else in the big wide world, except for your elixir and your fear of winding up back in jail.

Mais bon, as you would say; I can speculate myself to death wondering what you really thought of me and if and how much you liked me, since to you I was—sorry, if I'm repeating myself— not worth the paper I wasn't *written* on—or worth so much that you stopped yourself from leaving any *verifiable* trace. Were it not for my elephantine memory, in which our largely one-sided con- versations are stored as in a book, I'd have to imagine I'd merely dreamt everything and was still dreaming—and not only all the words we exchanged but also everything you did, or didn't do, with, for and against me.

Yet where the hell does that loutish arrogance on page nine come from, confirmed by your amateurish pencil drawings on pages ten, eleven and twelve, which present reasonable likenesses of your subjects with a viciousness at least equal to that in your texts?

Oh Harry, you hypocrite, whatever drove you to identify your admittedly more or less eager helpers not with a pseudonym or their initial, but by name? How am I supposed to continue to cherish my preferred hypothesis and believe that you withheld my name for my own protection? It would have been a simple task for any dumb cop, or even for the scarcely sharper lads on your side of the line, to identify me from keywords like Triad and the actual first names of our group. And why spare Marc from your boundless ingratitude? And what on earth, apart from good, did Joe, Clara, Marlene, Julia, Frank, Hanna, Thomas and Christoph ever do to you?! Why such spite towards people who were trying to help you and did help you, even if only for my sake?

OK, Clara was a flabby and thoroughly bad-natured cow whose every word people doubted, let alone that she had once pranced around provincial stages in a tutu. And it's true that she composed the most embarrassing and most heartless love poems, between ten and twenty a day at times, and she did torment us at every opportunity with ideological drivel sponsored by the Socialist Unity Party of West Berlin. But still: did she not bake bone-dry biscuits and make weak tea for you? Did she not drop you off to the very second for your therapy sessions, once even at eight in the morning?

And Marlene, who could trill her 'r's like a canary, took you out for hot-and-sour soup and on many evenings, as you once confessed, sang you to sleep—and may even occasionally have deprived you of it because by all indications you fancied her or, if not, you were the biggest hypocrite of all time.

And Juli, into whose 'green soft-toy eyes' you gazed far too deeply now and then? She gave you a silver chain she said she'd made herself and you've never removed it since. That wasn't the only reason I didn't like that stupid, lazy, sentimental, anorexic and otherwise wholly uncharismatic old bag.

And Frank, who didn't long to hear your prison anecdotes as you walked around together for hours, who bought you as much ice cream and coffee as you wanted and enough socks for three giant Brazilian millipedes, and to whom you never showed your nasty caricatures, quite possibly because you suspected how good *his* were. In those pictures of you—never naked, may I add—you looked alive: gutsy and disgruntled, sad and funny, smart and stupid, all at once.

And Hanna, who taught you to iron sheets and—as she supervised you—told you sardonic and nostalgic stories about Erfurt, the Thuringian city of her birth which to you seemed so far away, who acted out her parts for you and asked you if you liked the character she was rehearsing, taking you every bit as seriously as her evening audience?

It's true that Thomas and Christoph didn't really know how to deal with you, but that only became apparent later on and was due to something very serious that also only became apparent later. From then on, Clara, Marlene, Hanna and even Juli kept their distance from you, but Frank didn't nor Marc nor me, not even Joe who was the one who dropped the bombshell and could've dropped you—for the precise reason I'll return to later, as you know I will.

The two of us were in the Eisenacher Strasse half an hour before our appointment that Friday evening when our group was scheduled to meet for the first time. You were wearing the new 'anarchist black' shirt I'd bought you on the way there because you though it looked *si sophistiqué*, and I was carrying the bag with your old sweatshirt in it. As I peered anxiously towards the subway station, chain-smoking and occasionally wiping my sweaty palms on your broad back in its fluffy corduroy cladding, you played it cool, running a comb through your hair, chewing mints and stretching.

Everyone who had expressed a willingness did indeed turn up in good time, cast coy or inquisitive looks at you and one another, greeted me, asked hardly any questions and sauntered after us along the corridor to Joe's door, as if what awaited them behind it were merely some free adult-education taster course.

Joe let us in at seven on the dot and offered neither you nor me nor anyone else his hand. One of the three desks, presumably Joe's, had been pushed to one side; in its place, twelve chairs were arranged in a semi-circle.

'Well, good evening. If you'd all take a seat,' Joe said with studied nonchalance but, if I remember correctly, there was a glint in his eye, when his met mine, of something like knowing respect for me or at least for the organizational ambition I'd shown. Joe seemed to recognize that without someone this energetic, he would soon be out of his probably well-paid job for want of clients.

Joe didn't take a seat but, pacing up and down before us like a lecturer in an auditorium, he explained once again that he was 'Joe, plain Joe' and that there was a little money for you and then described the point of the therapy whose success depended on our 'commitment' and on sticking to 'the rules', which applied to you 'more than to anyone else here'. 'I know what I'm talking about,' Joe said. 'I shot a cool million's worth of dope into my veins and did a good long stretch in jail too. You, Harry, are right at the start, as I see it, not a day older than when you first shot up. You're twelve, thirteen at most, and nothing and nobody, just a stupid, grabbing, useless junkie . . . '

Here you interrupted Joe. 'What do you mean, "junkie"?' you crowed in a strangely reedy voice, half rising from your chair. 'I'm supporting the Kurdish freedom fighters.'

It's possible you thought this comment was funny, but only Clara laughed. Joe gave you a lingering and condescending look that said more than his accompanying words: 'All right, Harry.'

After an awkward silence, which even he didn't appear to enjoy, Joe asked us all to give our name, phone number, profession and 'hobbies', so you knew what you were in for. The only other question he had was whether we had any questions. We didn't; only Thomas enquired where and when we'd be receiving 'the wages for our efforts'. 'Once a month,' Joe announced, 'when we meet here. So make sure you note down your hours properly. And don't forget, the kid has to be on time. Any problems, just give me a call.'

As we were all smokers, we were glad Joe let us go again so soon. On the left at the next junction, in the Swan Lake Café, we ordered Cokes and beers and casually drew up the 'Harry plan' for the next two weeks. It was easier than I'd imagined, especially as it was already clear that you'd spend most weekends with me and I would always be willing to fill in if, once in a while, someone couldn't make it.

IX

Over the following period you were barely ever on your own. We took turns to drop you off at the therapy sessions, which you had to face alone with four other addicts we knew nothing more about or with a Triad employee, generally Joe. When you'd finished, whichever one of us was on duty would be waiting outside and you had to follow them wherever he—or she—wanted to go: to a cinema, a pub, a flat, his, hers, mine . . . You were no longer allowed out without a chaperone, not even to take the urine tests, although they were soon scheduled only every other day and sometimes not overseen by hawkeyed Joe but by a variety of interns.

The two of us virtually always made these morning trips to the Eisenacher Strasse, as the other groupies soon got into the habit of delivering or checking you in to my place, always on Saturdays and Sundays and sometimes for weeknights. I never asked why. Perhaps they couldn't cope with the responsibility while they slept or were frightened that you might eavesdrop on their love life, deplete their fridges, abscond with their wallets . . . Perhaps they simply imagined that it was with me, your steady girlfriend, that you'd be in the safest hands.

The first month went very well. We lived on my dole and what remained of the undeclared flower-dough after I'd paid off Christoph. When I didn't have to go with you to pee or you were otherwise assigned, I scrubbed the flat and then myself, made soup and waited for you and Clara, or you and Juli, or you and Frank, because they liked to come up with you for a plate of lentils or a glass of wine.

As soon as it was just the two of us again, we would watch TV, listen to Marlene's records or lie quietly in the dark; you drank your Coke, I my red wine. After the third bottle at the very latest, I would reach for your cock, which I considered mine. And one evening (I thought at first it was an acoustic hallucination) you called me 'babe'—and made life difficult for me. Clambering off you, I moaned: Don't call me that, don't call me babe!

'Why not?' you asked. 'Babies are pink, soft and sweet, just like you. And you smell a little of sour milk, my big, round babe.'

To which I replied: I'm not sour, I'm sore. Say anything else, just don't say babe.

But, Harry, you weren't listening but repeating that one stupid word over and over again: 'Babe, babe, babe . . . ' you said in a low voice, kissing the corners of my mouth so delicately that it left me speechless and almost breathless. You rolled me onto my back and at long last put your face between my legs. And the garbled noises I emitted against my will, if I retained anything of that description, sounded like a baby crying, so they didn't sound happy, even though *I* was.

By and by you fell asleep, after all you loved nothing better than sleeping; I stayed awake, though, thinking of something I'd experienced years earlier. That night, I thought the story was a parallel to yours, if not a response to it, and I wanted to tell you; but I never did. For although you never said anything, I got the impression over time that you didn't really care for stories, neither telling nor listening to them. —Now, Harry, I can no longer bore you, you can no longer drop off to sleep while I'm speaking, no longer walk out of the room in the middle of one of my sentences, come back to me a few minutes later and in your inimitable, gently dismissive way, ask: 'What now?'

It was a Saturday in October '63. I'd taken the subway in the morning to Königs Wusterhausen to pick mushrooms, though actually to shake off the gloom that had been weighing on my mood for days for no identifiable reason. Because it was raining, however, I didn't even make it to the edge of the forest but went into the station bar—and got stuck there.

The bar was full of men, weird men with twinkly eyes, although quite a few of them already seemed to be seeing double. And all of them were tattooed, some of them not just on their arms but on their hands and necks too, yes even on their faces. I learnt that the elongated deep-blue mark next to the right nostril of a rough chap called Wilhelm was a 'teardrop tattoo' and that these teardrops were only to be found on 'blokes' who'd 'done time'. —It's not unlikely, Harry, that your clown doll was only so suspect to me because of the painted droplet under one of its glass eyes; but maybe I'm only associating the two because I now remember Wilhelm and the words 'teardrop tattoo'.

He and most of the others gathered in the bar, Wilhelm told me, had been amnestied a week earlier to mark 'our most important public holiday' and released from the 'Regis-Breitingen opencast-lignite-mine penal institution' near Altenburg, and now it was a 'right booze-up' until the 'few measly quid' they had from the last three months' hard labour laying railway tracks were all gone and they were 'dead drunk'.

I didn't ask why he'd been inside, only why he was getting pissed in this particular station bar rather than heading into Berlin.

'We, meaning me and that lot over there,'—here Wilhelm (who had banned me from calling him Willy, yet steadfastly called me Sonya) jerked his thumb over his shoulder—'come from around here, and the landlord used to be one of us too. And anyway, where else are we supposed to go? You think our missuses have been waiting for us? Nuh, they're not standing at the stove in their negligees cooking us cabbage rolls, no chance.'

Wilhelm had strong shoulders, a flame-red farmer's face and old, glassy eyes. I can't remember if I got drunk with him because I fancied him or the other way round, only that I really lived it up, especially as, despite the brandy he kept ordering, Wilhelm neither broke character nor anything else, clinking his glass against mine with every fresh round and growling, 'Anyway, cheers, dear.'

Hours later, it was pitch-black outside and I was sufficiently plastered. Wilhelm, who had nipped to the bar and returned with a key in his hand, put his arm around me so tightly I couldn't stumble, let alone fall, and led me across the smoky pub towards a door. I didn't get the feeling that Wilhelm either desperately wanted or needed what was about to happen, but as conditions were favourable and I was there, it must have been part of the 'I'm out' ritual. Also, Wilhelm had liberally treated or invested in me, and after all I had to sleep somewhere—and had never done it with someone like him, who'd served years of hard labour but had now been pardoned and would be free for who knows how short a time.

Beyond the door lay a small, stuffy room. Yellow light seeped through a standard lamp's pleated shade on to the greenish rag covering the pulled-out sofa bed. Wilhelm didn't pretend to be a Lothario, didn't even look as I took off my sandals, blouse, skirt, bra and knickers. It was only when I sat down beside him, warming my bare thighs on his still trouser-clad ones, that he reached for me, not impetuously, not roughly, but with clumsy caution, as if I were a foreign body that might be easily damaged or even dangerous. Wilhelm's palms were dry and hard, his fingertips chapped, so each of his movements tickled a little; and when Wilhelm ran his hands down my back to the spot where it divided, I heard a crackle over the muffled but not excessively quiet bar noises that reached us through the bright gap at the top of the door. Eventually Wilhelm too removed his roll-neck sweater, undid his belt and his flies, manoeuvred me on to the edge of the sofa, prised my legs apart with his knees and, dumbly yet purposefully, to start with, like a blind, smooth creature with a mind of its own, his penis burrowed inside me. As he moved impatiently back and forth without really concentrating, I examined the blue, green and red drawings on his shoulders, his hairy chest and his arms. There were two flaming hearts, a ship, a sword, an empty gallows, a rose and a grinning tortoise I liked and tried to stroke; but Wilhelm's upper right arm, the tortoise's home, was bent so far away from me that I could only have reached it if I'd been able to sit up.

Was it that night I wanted to tell you about Wilhelm, or a different one? Once, however, I did ask you why you didn't have a single tattoo despite spending so much time in jail, and if that kind of thing maybe wasn't so common in West German prisons. You explained that over here only criminals 'inked one another'. However, because they had 'nicked' you for 'procurement offences' and addiction-motivated holdups, you had always considered yourself a leftie, not a 'crook'. Your goal had never been to get rich, only to 'provide for' yourself and people like you; and 'illegalizing' only the types of drugs from which the state couldn't make any money or didn't want to meant 'criminalizing left-wingers' and putting them on a par with 'common criminals', and that was utterly criminal because 'no violence should originate' from the state, not from one calling itself democratic in any case. Politicals, meaning anarchists, Red Army Faction members and other terrorists, also did long spells 'inside', but they 'quite consciously' didn't prick pretty pictures on each other, apart, maybe, from the dove of peace. But a Picasso-style dove-of-peace tattoo, which must bear some similarity to the wood pigeon—known less, ironically, for its remarkably un-dovelike aggressiveness than for its snow-white plumage—would be very hard to see unless it was on the skin of a Black Red, and so far you'd never met one of them, either inside nor outside.

Wilhelm had soon finished, and I was glad he had. He fell asleep—of course. I lay beside him against the cold wall for two or three hours, heard him snoring, felt thirsty and couldn't get comfortable. When the murmuring in the bar died away and there was only the sound of glasses banging against one another because, as I correctly surmised, the landlord was washing up, I got up from the bed, gathered my clothes, got dressed, opened the door and closed it again behind me.

'Mornin',' the landlord said.

'What time is it?' I asked.

His reply: 'Past three. The first train'll be leaving soon.'

It was raining harder than the day before. A glance at the timetable told me that I'd have to wait until ten to four. I stood shivering and dog-tired on the platform, which was covered, fortunately, not knowing whether I ought to sit down or not. On the one hand, I wanted to spread and stretch my legs out in front of me so I would no longer have to feel the wet, sticky stuff between them, but on the other hand I didn't want to catch a stronger whiff of the stale sperm odour emanating from my groin—if, that is, it wasn't already in the air. I was also worried that if I sank down on to one of the benches, I'd immediately fall asleep and miss the first train—or trains.

Although my tongue was furry and tasted of dead mouse, I still felt an urge to smoke. But there were neither cigarettes nor a lighter in my shoulder bag, only my purse, a mushroom knife, three folded paper bags and an almost empty box of matches. So I must have left an open packet of f6 in the bar or in the room behind it. I had enough time, so if my purse hadn't also been empty except for a few pennies I would certainly have gone back—(Where was the little money I'd had? Had I paid for a couple of rounds in a drunken fit of pride?)—not to Wilhelm, who was probably still snoring, but to get a new packet from the machine outside the pub.

So I wouldn't be able to smoke for quite a while; grasping this fact ramped up my craving to a level where I was wide awake and otherwise indifferent to the state I was in. I prowled along the platform, scouring every inch and the two stone dustbins for a nice-looking fag butt or perhaps an almost untouched cigarette just lit and then tossed away when the train pulled in and then gone out. I picked up two or three stubs, but they smelt so revolting that I dropped them again and had decided I'd rather tough it out for a few hours when down between the rails I spotted a soft pack of Club that had obviously slipped from someone's grasp and landed on its edge; it looked relatively full and several cigarettes were poking out of the opening by the excise stamp.

I raised my eyes to the grey sky and I would have prayed if I'd known how. My enthusiasm and my yearning were so great that I paid no mind to the gap between the platform and the tracks and simply jumped down.

My loot had been resting against the inside of the rail and so although the packet was a bit wet, the cigarettes weren't; well, maybe a little damp but otherwise fine. I struggled to control my urge to strike a match and light up right there, which was, I now discovered, a surprisingly long way down. Soon, I thought; soon I'll have my first drag. But it was the train that would be sooner, so I crammed the packet into my bag, grabbed hold of the platform edge—and hung there like sack of potatoes. My arms were feeble, and pull-ups had never been one of my few sporting strong suits. However hard I tried, I couldn't heave myself up far enough to brace my elbows on the concrete overhang and lever the rest of my body over the top. My futile efforts only drained my energy further, and this cruel weakness was coupled with my fear of the time, the moment when I'd hear it approaching—the first train of the day.

But what I actually heard, coming quickly closer with loud, booming thuds, was the clatter of many feet—human feet, as it turned out; to be precise, the feet of men in blue uniform. When the clatter stopped and I looked up, I saw heads—heads with peaked caps and, under the cap peaks, furious faces. Two large hands grabbed my arms roughly and pulled me up with an ease that left me puzzled but not rejoicing, because I realized whom I was going to have to deal with and what would happen next. No sooner was I up than the train pulled in; one of the five uniformed men (if I interpreted their epaulettes and cap bands correctly, two of them were transport police) swiftly twisted my right arm behind my back, so hard that a lancing pain ran through my shoulder joint, then pushed me along in front of him and down the stairs and through the dark underpass reeking of ammoniac and, reaching the end of the tunnel, into an office lit by a flickering fluorescent tube.

The officer who had pulled me up and led me away, a tall, stocky man of about thirty, let go of my arm and shoved me in the chest, which made me throw my head back and look at him. 'You're a total idiot,' he roared.

The other four were clustered around us, very close to me and to one another, something I only noticed because I didn't want to return the howler monkey's gaze a second time, so I looked past him. The next moment, I couldn't see anything; my skull filled with water, which rose higher and higher until it started pouring from my eyes and nostrils as if I were a badly tangled hose attached to a running tap that had sprung its first four leaks after pressure had worn it thin. I sobbed and sniffed and panted and heard nothing outside my body until, in a barely intelligible high-pitched voice that sounded foreign even to me, I asked if I could smoke. A hand gripped my chin. The man whose hand it was, or someone else, said, 'Chin up'. Someone ran a hand over my hair, passed me a checked handkerchief and pushed a chair under my knees and a lit cigarette between my lips. A voice sighed, 'Come on, girl, you're still so young'; and I carried on crying, and the cigarette tasted like fried rubber.

The wind had changed, and the railway police's anger had gone up in smoke faster than this first of many cigarettes they gave me. With the exception of the one who'd pulled me up and dressed me down, not one of the men looked younger than forty, which perhaps explains why my tears had stirred up fatherly feelings in them, and had in any case moved them to assume that it was heartbreak that had made me first get drunk and then take to the tracks.

'It's OK, little girl,' one of them said. 'Forget that arsehole. He's no reason to kill yourself. You could have any man you want, because you'd be so pretty if you would only stop blubbing and wash yourself.'

Another man fished out a rectangular half-litre bottle of brandy from the inside pocket of his jacket. 'Me and Rolf here,' he said, pointing to the fat man next to him, 'are about to go off duty, so we're going to treat ourselves to a drop.' And Rolf opened a metal locker on the opposite wall, took out three glasses and set them down on the desk.

'She should have a bite to eat first, though, the state she's in,' said the tall skinny man whom I reckoned was one of the two transport police. He stood up, went over to the shelves behind me, came back with a bread tin, from which he dug out half a tangy-smelling sandwich, and a thermos flask whose lid he filled with steaming black coffee.

I ate the pâté sandwich, drank the coffee and the brandy and then another and another, and my tears stopped flowing. No, no, I said quietly and very nicely as if I now had to console these men; I'm not heartbroken, I didn't want to die, just have a smoke; and down there on the track bed were what I was missing, you know, these here. I showed the five men, a little triumphantly, the packet of Club I'd finally managed to claw out of my shoulder bag but hadn't yet smoked because I was so nicely provided for.

And now the wind changed again; the fire of kindness went out in the eyes all around me, and it was I who had extinguished it. Fat Rolf, whose was the first gaze to turn to ashes, removed the thermos flask from the table and then the brandy bottle, which he pointedly screwed shut before hissing to the quiet room: 'You must be joking. Are you pulling our legs, you little toad, trying to make us believe you'd risk your neck for a few smokes? Well, that won't work with me. Take a deep breath because now you're in trouble. *Big* trouble.'

I glimpsed how foolish, indeed dangerous it was to try to tell the truth in this situation and in the hands of these public officials. And anyway, what was the truth? Has anyone ever been free of heartache? After the onset of puberty, wasn't any heartache a form of heartbreak?

I don't know if these kinds of questions crossed my mind back then in that railway workers' common room or only when I was lying beside you, unable to tell you this story. Or are they only bubbling up now because I'm preoccupied by both stories, the one that took place back then in Königs Wusterhausen, and ours, which won't be finished until I'm finished too?

Rolf snatched my shoulder bag, which was strictly speaking a shapeless, stained, once-yellow leather pouch, tipped its contents out onto the table, grabbed the purse in which he suspected my identity card would be—or some other document providing a clue to my identity—but found nothing save my last three pennies and a subway ticket stamped the previous day. He turned my bag completely inside out, and fluff and a few pine needles trickled out of the holey taffeta lining. 'Do you have pockets in your skirt and something in them to prove your identity?' Rolf asked.

Despite being fully aware of the impending danger I lost control of myself for a second. It might have been all the drinks I'd knocked back in quick succession, but whatever it was, I giggled and traced circles on the table with the index finger of my dirty left hand and replied: Of course I do. Look, here's my ticket. That's what you're supposed to check, isn't it?'

This was too much for the man called Rolf and the other four, because they said nothing for a long time until one of them turned to the small shelf in the corner on which, as I only now noticed, stood a grey telephone. Rolf picked up the receiver, weighed it in his hand like a cudgel, cleared his throat and said in an almost emotionless voice: 'That's enough. Name, address, age?'

Sorry, I didn't mean to be cheeky, I wailed. Soya's my name, Soya Edith Krüger, home address Karl-Marx-Allee 112, I turned sixteen in March this year, Class 10 b at Carl von Ossietzsky High School.

'Oh no you don't,' said the somewhat younger man who had pulled me up. 'You're not winding us up again. Rolf, dial the number for the registration office in Mitte . . . Damn,' he broke off, 'it's too early. I'll take this little devil down to the local police station. Who's coming along?'

One man only, presumably the boss, indicated that he had to stay. Rolf put his hand on the back of my neck; I knew that neither tears nor cockiness would help me now and, as with many people in a clinch, it was my mother who came to mind, my mother with whom I had a difficult relationship even then and indeed from the very start. She thought I was a failure, I thought she was heartless, a workaholic who, if she wished, could sew great clothes—and play battle songs on the piano accordion, something I found intensely embarrassing. Even more embarrassing, though, was the political ambition that puffed her up a little more every day; and once, when she was biting into a salami as she crouched in front of the fridge, I crept up behind her and startled her by shouting, You're going to burst soon—with pride. She climbed the career ladder as singlemindedly as she'd once climbed that weeping willow by the lake. The buxom devotee of the Free

German Youth with a deep Saxon-accented voice, in which she would proclaim the stupidest clichés, had risen to a position of party official, and I didn't dare imagine what she might become and would become if everything followed its usual socialist course because it scared me; only for my own sake, mind you, because I was undeniably this woman's flesh and blood. In short, I was ashamed—in front of her and of her.

I knew that time was running out to avoid the worst, and despite or because of that, a sentence suddenly whizzed out like a comet from the dark void between the few dots of light inside my skull and hurtled towards my tongue, a sentence that had come to me once in a dream and woken me up because I'd regarded it as an epiphany, the solution to a problem I had only dreamt of and long since forgotten: Call my mother so she can help me, then kill her. It wasn't this sentence that crossed my lips, though, for what I said instead was: Well, guess who my mother is. Her name's Alma Krüger. Comrade Krüger, second secretary of the regional leadership, in case you need reminding. Now get your hands off me or *you*'ll be the ones in trouble.

Rolf's grip relaxed, as if someone had shot him with a stun gun. His hand went dead and slid off my neck and a little way down my back. Then the contact between his body and mine was broken, for ever I hoped—though I felt no relief. I was hot and my face must have been red as a cooked prawn from shame. I didn't dare look at anyone, but even so I knew they knew what I knew; that after this 'coming out', as they say nowadays, once I'd dropped my mother's name, every further word spoken against me could have nasty consequences; that even if, in spite of their different ranks, they were to stick up for one another and describe the events with one voice, there would be blots on their records that could never be expunged, and that although there were five of them and I was alone, credence would only be given to my version, yes *given*, because the police officers, members of the arbitration committee, judges, etc. who would decide on the case would *have* to believe me because I was Alma Krüger's daughter.

Neither I nor anyone else knows whether and why they believed what I had been forced to divulge, only that it was clear to all six of us how incriminating a single whisper of doubt regarding the truth of my as yet unproved assertion might turn out to be. When I glanced over at the shelf, the receiver was back on its hook, and I lowered my boiling head again, and the icy silence was broken by the creak of the door, which one of the men had opened—and held open until I'd disappeared past him and out into the dark underpass.

Only when I had come to the platform and to myself, bathed in sweat, as if waking from an anaesthetic or a dream, did I notice that I had left the packet of Club down in the office. But then the train pulled in and pulled me away with it—to Schönhauser Allee station, the long street where my friend Claudia lived and, if she was at home, she would give me two or three cigarettes and maybe even lend me some money.

X

The day came when Joe had convened us for the second time. The intervening period had flown past and was, compared to the one that now commenced, more pleasant and carefree than any moment since.

You hadn't spent the night before that Friday, 22 May 1987, in my bed or, as had been increasingly the case over the previous two weeks, at least in my flat, but in Juli's spare bed, unless that was yet another lie.

So shortly before noon I travelled to Charlottenburg to pick you up. I was sure that you would be shaved and dressed and happy to see me, especially as I planned to invite you—and even Juli—to a restaurant that served your favourite meal, stuffed cabbage; the best in the city, apparently. But you were still sitting in a dressing gown, Juli's dressing gown, on that spare bed, a faded red velvety sofa you had hauled out of a pile of rubbish in the street and restored fairly competently. Juli, who had opened the door in nothing but some kind of lilac-coloured negligee, slouched back down next to you behind the coffee table, which was empty apart from the ashtray and two, not three, little gold-rimmed glasses filled with cream liqueur. You'd had a late breakfast, she said. Although you barely touched your glass and let me drink it, you too said you weren't in the mood for any 'solids'. I felt rotten, like an intruder, a spoilsport. In a deliberately casual tone of voice that made me sound like a repentant crook and reminded me, and probably you two, of Joe, I asked you to get a move on, quick, and, after you had disappeared into the bathroom, asked Juli to be stricter with you, more understanding of me and punctual from then on.

Juli's glazed green gaze rested on me with unwavering mildness. 'Oh Soya,' she said, 'love is like measles. You only get it once and the later it happens, the worse it is. Tolstoy, I think.'

I bit back a reply, as I couldn't think of one that wouldn't have given me away, but above all because I was afraid of Joe speaking through my lips again.

I was still close to tears as we walked to the subway. I hung on to your right arm, heavier than the bag of potatoes I'd bought at a Turkish shop in Juli's street because we weren't going to eat out after all; and next to a newspaper stand I gave you little kisses behind your ear, which you accepted as apologies. And your mood improved; in the train you laughed as you cradled the two-kilo net of potatoes on your lap. 'These are potatoes from clever farmers.'

When I stared blankly at you, you laughed even harder. If the stupidest farmers always grew the biggest potatoes, you explained, then our small ones must come from clever growers. 'Man, they must be so smart and hardworking to produce these tiddlers from ordinary spuds. Mind you, the ultimate goal must be pea potatoes. You'll only need to boil them for three minutes and then you can eat them with the skins on.'

Tears, albeit tears of laughter, ran down your face, not mine, when you saw not a twitch at the corners of my mouth. You looked at me, then back at the wrinkly, already germinating potatoes, which you said were making eyes at you, and just carried right on laughing.

Back home, I forced you down onto my mattress; you cooperated, still laughing. You must have been flattered by how much I wanted you—and to keep you inside me until the end this time. But when I had come, quickly as usual and violently under the pressure of jealousy or for fear of losing you or both, you succeeded once again in fetching me down from the pole, which was how I too had started to refer to your interruption method. You slid your large hands under my armpits as if we were practising a gymnastics routine, and lifted me away from you. But I didn't want to float in mid-air. My thighs clenched you in a vice-like grip; I shifted all my substantial weight onto your cock, which I clearly felt go limp and shrink—and though this aroused me more than the already waning orgasm had, I was quite powerless to prevent it. This feeling of powerlessness was so overwhelming that I was afraid I might be paralysed by an inextricable bout of cramp. It is possible that you sensed this because while one of your hands held me even more tightly, the fingers of your other hand caressed the spot above my tummy where I was most ticklish. And the paralysis that had gripped me and begun to stiffen my muscles relaxed and changed me again: into a twitching, giggling ball, which eventually rolled off you and around the mattress for a while. By then you had draped the dressing gown around you and gone off to the kitchen.

You soon came back, as you always did while we lived together. Clutching a spoon between your teeth and a bowl of yoghurt in front of your chest, you sat down, looked at me as if you meant to say something and opened your mouth, but only to drop the spoon into the yoghurt pot. A cute trick which I otherwise admired; this time, though, its sole effect was to sober me up.

You and Frank left my flat before me that morning because the two of you wanted to pick up some wood somewhere. So I went to Eisenacher Strasse without you. In the staircase, at the near end of the long hallway leading to the Triad's offices, I came across four women who, Joe admitted five minutes later in response to my questioning, had just been at the 'family group'. One of the women barred my path, examining me with such hostility that I couldn't help asking what was bugging her.

'We', she grumbled, 'are the mothers of the people who end up here. We didn't choose our children. But what is it with bimbos like you, eh? Are you a pervert or can you just not find a better boner?'

Isn't that a bit simplistic, I replied, more tersely than I'd intended, and squeezed past the women, scraping my backside along the wall.

Again we sat there on our folding chairs like good pupils, and again Joe paced up and down for a few anxiety-inducing minutes before speaking, examining us closely, one after the other, then enquiring with studied indifference, as if he were enquiring about the weather in Vladivostok, how things were going 'with our Harry'.

For a few minutes, which stretched on for what felt like an eternity, there was silence. Everyone other than me smiled wanly and looked in every direction except at Joe.

Clara finally cleared her throat after Joe's gaze had alighted on her. 'Oh, what the hell,' she said falteringly and as if you weren't in the room. 'Harry's had very little contact with educated people who are politically and culturally active in recent years, which is why he often doesn't have an opinion of his own. At least he knows what doesn't interest him and he can listen, up to a point. It takes time to learn to understand poetry, and Harry would need someone like me, and then one day it'll click because he isn't stupid. I wouldn't mind a bit more communication, but I do enjoy teaching him. He has to want it, though. The two months we have left aren't long, just long enough to make a start, which will soon be behind us, thank God . . . '

Clara could probably have carried on with this guff and if she, of all people, hadn't responded to Joe's prompting, the rest of us wouldn't have spoken at all.

'Oh, give over with that bollocks about poetry,' Frank cut in. 'We get by. Harry's already made picture frames with me and packed up an entire exhibition on his own, more or less. His only flaw is that he he'd rather get it wrong than ask.'

'Not everything,' Hanna intervened. 'Harry's great at making sandwiches, cooking instant soup and folding the washing, no questions asked.'

'We listen to music a lot. It's easy and incredibly relaxing, especially given that Harry's life's pretty stressful at the moment,'

Marlene chipped in, and I wanted to speak after her and lavish a bit more praise on you in a way I believed to be therapeutically astute; for example, your social skills, your little gifts, your calm, thoughtful manner . . .

But Joe got there first. 'Do you think Harry's honest? Does he ever talk about himself? Does he say how he's feeling, what's up with him? And has any of you shown an interest and expressed that interest? Do you have any idea, my dear dwarves and substitute dwarves, about the man who's been sleeping in your beds, eating off your plates and drinking from your cups these past few weeks? He isn't Snow White, but there's still poison involved.'

Having stopped in front of your chair, Joe now stepped closer to you and shoved you quite hard in the chest with the heels of his hands. 'Come on, Harry,' he hissed quietly but sharply, 'get up off your arse and tell them. You obviously haven't found the courage to do so yet, so tell them now, right away.'

You stayed seated though, bowed your head and went red, something I alone could see clearly because your chair was at the end of the row—and mine to the right of it—and I was leaning far enough towards you for my hair to brush your knees. Within seconds there were beads of sweat on your forehead; and unless I was hallucinating, at least one of them dripped onto my face before I could pull it away.

You kept silent. We held our breath. Bobbing around in front of you like a footballer about to take the first penalty, or a police inspector waiting to hear a long-overdue confession, Joe badgered you: 'Come on, out with it. We haven't got all day.'

You remained stubbornly silent and doubled over even further on your chair.

'All right,' Joe said when you could no longer make yourself any smaller, 'so you can't bring yourself to come clean. You're not willing to confront your friends, without whom you'd have been back on dope and back in prison weeks ago, with the fact that you're HIV-positive?'

I could find no words, neither in the following days nor later, Harry, for the feeling Joe's words provoked in me. I'll find it hard, even now, to express my emotions back then. It was as if I'd been injected with a cocktail of fear, disappointment, anger and self-pity, a cocktail that made an immediate and powerful impact but failed to numb me entirely. It was like an electric shock adminis-tered by fate, an explosion inside my skull that threatened to blow my mind while simultaneously sharpening it. The roar and rumble in my ears was so loud that I heard the remark Joe had elicited from you as a high-pitched howl, underscoring rather than punc-tuating the thunderstorm, although it may only have been the wind; it was as if I heard not the words you or Joe or someone else spoke, not the sounds that drilled into my head from left and right, front and back, above and below, but my own thoughts wailing like babies woken from their slumbers.

'So what . . . only found out myself a couple of weeks ago . . . got hepatitis B and C too . . . you repress things, you know . . . Joe, you snitch . . . it's enough to make a sheep turn bad . . . ': those are roughly the phrases I remember from what you said, that or something similar.

Being able to think would be fine if you didn't have to feel. Having to die while being of sound mind is barbaric, unreasonable. Using smack certainly makes it quicker but also easier. When I'm high, there are enough thrills, bad ones and good, and I'm forced to give my body what it needs so my head feels better—they're accomplices not separated by my neck but joined by it. What, apart from a few snacks, would I put in if my organism weren't there just to make sure there's some crackle and pop in my brain or at least some peace and quiet? And now Joe goes and claims it's my work of a lifetime to call time on this life. The idiot should try telling other idiots that crap, not me.

Do you remember how, while you were still stammering, Joe peered at his watch and instructed us with a sadistic grin to make sure we engaged our brains but gave yours 'a good wash once in a while'? Could you ever forget the panic in our eyes? Can you still hear the door slamming—like a slap in the face—when Joe kicked us out after precisely one hour? 'Good luck, everyone. See you next time. Chin up.'

Hanna gathered up her three full shopping bags and, like Christoph and Thomas before her, stormed off without so much as a glance at you, me, Joe or her husband who, with a smouldering cigarette clamped between his lips, waddled along the corridor at a peculiarly slow pace, like a badly wound-up mechanical duck, apparently so dazed that he didn't even notice the no-smoking signs plastered on both walls. Clara, around whose shoulders I reluctantly laid my arm for a second—lending her support I may have needed myself—was weeping silently into one of the crochet-edged handkerchiefs I'd mocked a few days earlier. Having previously avoided each other, Marlene and Juli were now holding hands. And for the first time I noticed what expressionless faces they could adopt; their faces were usually completely different but were now suddenly alike—and like those of the two stuffed pine martens which, along with other rotting specimens in the biological display case at my East Berlin school, I had once had to dust and rub with mink oil, of all things, as a punishment for 'disturbing lessons'. Only Marc the substitute, who had probably been with you more often than Christoph and Thomas, acted cool and indeed sought to establish contact with me and with Frank, Clara, Juli and Marlene, insisting, 'Come to the Swan Lake Café, please. We need to discuss how to carry on. And Harry probably wants to explain a few things.' *Harry*—even though I was constantly thinking of you, if what was going through my head qualifies as thinking, it was only at this cue that I realized you were missing. Clara, Juli and Marlene also stopped, turned and looked for the guilty party, for you.

You were crouching down motionless outside Joe's door, staring, as if you'd never seen it before, at the entrance to the men's toilets diagonally opposite, where for weeks you had filled cylindrical jars under supervision. Get a move on, man, I shouted. It sounded so shrill and mean that the others jumped and so did I, but it did startle you out of your paralysis.

Eventually we were all gathered around a table in the cafe, intensifying the already Edward Hopper–like atmosphere there—seven white-faced figures doing Swan Lake total justice, although no one, not even the ex-modern dancer Clara, felt like dancing and, other than the waitress, there was no audience.

Marc sat down to your left, deliberately leaving the chair between you free and, without anyone's approval or objection, ordered a round of vodkas and a bottle of water, then rested his head on the table top to be able to look at, and maybe even into, your eyes and said: 'This is total bullshit.'

I was frazzled, incapable of even thinking of thinking, and yet I still know that Marc's words sounded odd, ambivalent, duplicitous, vague (none of those adjectives is quite right), like sober analysis and timid reproach rolled into one; listening to their lingering echo, I focused entirely on you, as if only you could distract me from yourself. As I was wondering if you were even capable of feeling my and Marc's gazes, if you would answer him, perhaps with a wave at least, it took me a while to realize that Clara, Juli and Marlene were staring at *me*. It was only when the waitress, who had obviously cottoned on to the explosive nature of the situation, set down a jug of tap water, two different types of glass and a half-full bottle of Moskovskaya with barely a sound that I turned briefly away from you towards Juli. The look on Juli's face was like Marc's earlier words: ambivalent and vague—or like my look at you; I tried to console myself by viewing your problem as greater than mine, and Juli seemed to consider mine to be greater than hers, which seemed to numb her somewhat. There are moments when pity is less painful than self-pity. In any case, Juli's expression, with its mixture of fear and compassion, temporarily dispelled my suspicion that you two had been having a secret affair.

There was greater detachment in the way Clara and Marlene looked at me. They seemed to see me as no less dangerous than you, and their pupils focused on me one moment and then slid briskly left and right like the balls on a Russian abacus, suggesting that in their minds they were running through their potentially contagious situations with you and me. Were they thinking of kisses hello and goodbye, coffee cups, sheets, towels, smoker's cough . . . ?

We knew so little about this new disease at the time; nothing, in fact, apart from what had been printed in various papers for weeks and weeks about an impending pandemic, that it wasn't only transmitted sexually, that gay people were at a higher risk than others, that AIDS led to a swift and inevitable death . . . And I had no idea what a junkie was before I met you.

When Clara had cried some more, the brandy bottle was empty, Juli was drunk, Marlene feeling sick and Marc had abandoned his efforts, I paid the bill and, partly because your silence forced me to take the initiative, I bowed my head and made a short and, as soon became clear, not particularly convincing speech. Other than sex, nothing was really bad, and in any case it was worst for you, and deserting you now would be even worse. I said they should please, please ring me tomorrow and carry on, officially at least. I would take care of everything else . . .

'You're such an amazingly stupid cow,' Marlene interrupted, leaping out of her chair and gesticulating with both arms; her eyes glinted, her nostrils quivered, her cold fingers brushed my hand. Then, without another word, without a smile or a wave, she walked over to the door like a sleepwalker and out of it.

The rest of us also left, each alone, only me with you. The fact that you had to spend the remainder of that evening and half the following day in my care was part of our Harry plan, not part of the tacit agreement of whose full details I wasn't yet aware. Would some of them pull through, or would everyone jump ship at once? Who might still be inveigled into continuing or at least coming to the last group meeting? Or would you soon have to go back to jail because most of your groupies would avoid bidding you and me farewell tomorrow and instead inform Joe over the phone, and it would all be over? Through these kinds of absurdly practical questions, I tried to ward off the terror that filled me whenever I left myself the slightest pause for thought. I was exhausted, though, and soon I would have to stop resisting and lie down, and then it would hit me with full force, the terror would flood into me, drown me and sweep me away from you.

You were as silent as the grave while we walked to the subway station, during the journey, on the way to our street and even inside my flat. I didn't say anything either. Even the kitchen radio, whose dial you used immediately to twiddle until you found some music to your liking, remained off. I uncorked a bottle of red wine and sat down, as you did on the chair opposite me. After emptying my third glass in silence, I began to weep. The tears poured out of me like water; I sobbed, sniffed and groaned—and couldn't imagine it would ever stop. You didn't go away, but neither did you move any closer to me.

So that's why, I said after I don't know how much time had passed, that's why you fetch me down from the pole each time.

That's why I wasn't allowed to give you a . . . I couldn't bear to pronounce the word 'blowjob', finding it suddenly so funny that I began to laugh while blithely continuing to cry. If *that* wasn't hysterical, Harry, what was it?!

You got up, fetched the butter, salami and tomatoes from the fridge, made some sandwiches and opened the next bottle of red wine for me, all the time making sounds that you perhaps intended to soothe me. 'Psst, psst,' you hissed, as if you were dealing with a whining baby and not with your desperate girlfriend who believed she was dying, if only, for the time being, from fear.

XI

The next day, I was woken up by the sun warming my face; it was shining through the top right-hand corner of the window, and I guessed that it was twelve o'clock or later. I was covered up to the neck and—once more—still had my dress on. When I looked to one side and up, I saw you bending over me like a weeping willow in a dressing gown; your head was bowed, and your arms were hanging long and limp like an ape's so that they almost brushed me. Next to your bare feet was a tray with fresh rolls, jam and coffee on it. You had already rung Joe, you said to my face, which must have revealed how fast yesterday's events had come back to me, and he thought we should calm down and somehow things would carry on. He'd said that we had enough time before our farewell meeting. The real difficulties would only begin afterwards, and only for you.

Sure, Harry, I answered. Putting your own prospects first as always, even if you no longer actually have any. Am I to understand that you want to spend your final months free? What's going to happen to me though? What about the others? Don't you give a shit about them?

You sat down beside me. 'There's nothing to fear', you reckoned, 'you can take the test, if you like, but what for? Everything's fine.' You'd found your tongue again; you were almost chatty by your standards. It didn't matter if I didn't want to touch you any more. You could do without that, but not without my 'solidarity'.

You honestly had the nerve, on that day of all days, in that situation, to use that word, and it drove me up the wall rather than onto your pole. I sat up, kicked the covers and then the breadbasket away and stormed off to the kitchen. I stood for a long time in the shower under the warm jet of water, you waited outside it with a red towel open and ready and called with a laugh, 'Peace!'

Without so much as looking at you or the red towel, I stamped, dripping, back into the bedroom to dry myself on one of your scattered shirts but then decided against it, pulled on not my crumpled dress but a different one because I didn't want to go back into the kitchen, and slipped out without a thought for the therapy rule stating that we would not let you out of our sight for a minute. I hoped I would come to my senses, find a solution and reach a decision once I was out in the street on my own.

Oh, Harry; at this point, I've reached the subject of what was bound to come, my courage has vanished and I very much doubt I'll be able to do what I want to do—to tell you everything; I wonder if I should stop groping for words. This whole time I've been telling this story as best I can; but as for the dread that gripped me then and still haunts me now, which leaps for my throat like a dog whenever I think of that day at Joe's, that one meaningful and meaningless word is the only one that is even remotely adequate. No image, no symbol, no sound can replace or add to it or even describe it to you so that you might be exposed to it as I was and still am. Would I be able to describe this dread better (the word sounds harmless, unlike its rhyming colour) if I no longer felt it? Is it a matter of distance? Even though my focus is solely on bringing home to you what I felt and feel, I lack the necessary composure. It is the unconquerable dread itself that still leaves me speechless, again and again; especially as I haven't noticed the same thing in you, not at all. And if you felt some of that dread yourself, you never let it show.

And sometimes I think there was only one reason you resumed what, on one page in your notebook, you jokingly referred to as your 'hobby': you wanted me finally to have a—from your perspective—more real, more tangible reason to cry, for there to be a form of pain that enticed me away from the dread. I was meant to be more scared by your relapse into addiction than by the disease, about which all that anyone knew at the time was that it was insidious, developed stealthily and stigmatized those affected by it even before the long illness set in; and anyway, I was supposed to be more afraid for you than for myself. You were, of course, already familiar with the problems of getting hold of dope before you embarked—were forced to embark—on the experiment with us; those problems offered you some kind of grip, were perhaps your sole purpose in life; in any case, they curbed the fear of death that would probably have sooner or later overwhelmed you if you'd stayed clean. The stress—old for you, new to me—of scraping together enough money, avoiding going cold turkey, building up stashes, tricking probation officers and dodging cops took your mind off things. Why shouldn't it be the same for me?!

I don't know how Joe found out. From the prison doctor? Or can they tell from your piss now too? It's just like that arsehole to keep it under wraps and then lay a trap for me. But one day I'll be through with his pantomime or out of jail where the scumbag's dying to put me back. The game isn't up yet, although things aren't looking so rosy for me now. If need be, I can gather up my bits and bobs and do a runner. There are still a few tarts around just waiting for me to pull down the stockings they keep their savings in. And if none is handy, something else is bound to turn up. But I swear on my mother's grave that no one's just going to lock me up again.

I wandered through Moabit like a ghost, seeing nothing of what I saw—or actually I did: people were waiting under their umbrellas at a bus stop; to me they seemed unaware of how lucky they were. Otherwise I found my way but no way out of this mess—and I met no one and nothing that might have helped me decide. But what was that decision about?

In a pub I'd entered only because I was completely drenched, I sat down by the window, ordered a large beer, drank it mechanically and stared at the windowpane as if trying to hypnotize the water droplets running down the outside. I realized that I didn't feel like a second beer and had forgotten my purse, waited until the barman went through the stupid colour plastic strip curtain into the kitchen beyond, and then left without paying.

Only several side streets further on did I stop in front of a pet shop and look at a cage full of bulbous red-beaked zebra finches, huddling side by side on their perches. I couldn't tell for a second whether the soft cheeping I could feel rather than hear was coming from them or from my own lungs, which were not used to inhaling and exhaling so deeply.

I walked on for a while, sat down on a bench opposite the over-grown flowerbed between Turmstrasse and Stromstrasse and aban-doned myself to the storm of conflicting, ever-changing, alternately fading and flaring, forever inconclusive thoughts:

My money was with you in my flat or somewhere else, since you had to go to the Triad . . . After that, Marlene was due to pick you up and drop you back at my place for the night. Would she come though? I hadn't rung her, and she hadn't rung me. So until you'd finished your urine test and therapy session, I would sit in the Swan Lake Café—or not. Joe demanded absolute punctuality, but how was he supposed to check whether one of us was always and constantly with you? If all the others dropped out now and I was the only one left, then I would have to be your round-the-clock shadow. Was that possible? Wouldn't I have to take you along to the flower stall too, like Franz and his fat dog Bumblebee? Did I really want that now? No, I wanted to crawl into a hole, listen to my heartbeat, cry, feel each of my lymph nodes individually every three minutes and wait to come down with a fever. But was it likely that you'd infected me? Hadn't I been generally lucky in life and didn't I also have a strong constitution? Didn't your sexual precautions, which no longer seemed so strange, give me hope that I would emerge from this unscathed? 'Hope,' my grandma often said, 'is death.' And what next? I loved you, but did I also lust after you now I knew what you had? And even if I did lust after you, would I be able to kiss you, at least, without constantly won-dering whether I had a tiny crack in my lip, my tongue or my gum; and if I didn't, would you? Would I get used to condoms and overcome my fear which, despite the precautions I too would henceforth be required to take, overshadowed all other emotions?

With panic constantly breathing down my neck, would I ever have another orgasm? With you? And if another man approached me the day after tomorrow or in the future and I fancied him, what would I do? How would I put him off? Did I still feel any passion or desire? Not right now I didn't; not even for a little masturbation in Christoph's bath. And should such urges ever materialize again, wouldn't it be a good thing, not only for me and whichever man it was, if the ever-present fear made him beat a hasty retreat? And what if I were infected despite your 'precautions'? What did I stand to lose, other than my life? I couldn't catch it again, so at least I could still have sex with you. I would be what I'd never previously been beyond an undefined point—faithful. I would die, if not from fear—or in a traffic accident of the usual kind or from its after-effects—then from this damn disease, poor and miserable, and unfortunately only after you had died. Or not unfortunately? If you were dead and I was deeply distressed but not yet too much of an invalid, then I could find someone else if necessary, someone who had AIDS too . . .

It is unlikely I would have been able to extract myself from these torturous thoughts if pressing events had not prevailed: I had to go back to my flat to check you were still there, you and my purse. I had to try to get in touch with Marlene and ask her if she was coming to pick you up or if yesterday had ended her involvement, and then, whatever she said, it would once more be time to head to the subway.

You weren't at home, but my purse was lying where I suspected it was, in the drawer of the kitchen table, and when I checked, not a single banknote was missing, though maybe a few coins were. Then I spotted your note on the fridge: 'Gone on my own. See you later, Harry.'

I interpreted 'Gone on my own' as a sign that you were on your way to Eisenacher Strasse and so I relaxed a bit, even though you had never previously broken the therapeutic rules, not when setting out from my place anyway. But hadn't it just crossed my own mind too that we might gradually adopt a slightly more flexible approach to Joe's guidelines?

I phoned Marlene, who said she would 'pick you up on time', to ask you a couple of questions, if nothing else. Whether she carried on or not would depend on your answers—if, that is, you had any for her today. 'You don't need to explain yourself. I believe you when you say you had no idea what kind of mess you were getting us all into,' she said calmly and made some excuse to hang up.

I dialled the other groupies' numbers but couldn't get through to any of them, decided that this was hardly surprising in the middle of the day and plopped down on my mattress, somewhat relieved that I didn't need to speak to anyone. I was so tired and wanted on the one hand to slip away, on the other to continue my brooding and hear you come at some point—I mean, in through the door; I'd long since given you a key. The question of what was worse, staying awake and thinking, or sleeping and dreaming, was the cat chasing its tail that finally plunged me into the twilight zone.

XII

When did you come home? Had Marlene been able to have a word with you and accompany you to my front door afterwards? What woke me again that night? You switching on the lights? More likely, it was the feeling of something moving on my covers, something lighter and faster and completely unlike a human hand. Before I even caught sight of it, I knew that the thing walking around on me couldn't be your fingers. Yet only when the pattering stopped for a few seconds and I sensed the weight of a small creature on my chest, followed by a peculiar tickling sensation at the corner of my mouth, caused by something feathery, did I open my eyes without realizing, because it was so close, that I was being snuffled by a small animal. I shook my head, surprised rather than disgusted; I didn't think I was dreaming—who dreams of being tickled?—when suddenly the animal leapt to one side as if startled and I could finally see what it was: a rat, a small or still very young black rat with gleaming black eyes and long, gently quivering whiskers on its white muzzle, and white paws and a white patch on its tummy, as I soon discovered because it stood up on its hind legs, raising its nose to sniff the air—and won my heart from a standing start, so to speak.

You grabbed the rat, which clearly didn't mind this kind of treatment. My eyes followed it until it was sitting on your shoulder and its button eyes were gazing down at me, as were yours.

'He's a Scandinavian white-footed rat—none of your ordinary canal-dwellers. I bought him in the pet shop on Mierendorffplatz. His name is Salammbô,' you said in a curiously fatherly tone of voice, 'but it's written and pronounced Salaam-bô because "salaam" is Arabic for "peace", if you see what I mean.'

I remember you waiting for me outside the shower that morning in a matador pose, waving the red towel and crying 'Peace', and I mumbled, All right, I'll call him Salaam. And by the way, I don't care much for the Orient, but Salammbô is a girl's name. Salaam would be better for a boy. Not that I'm going to be writing to him, mind.

'OK, but if you do, I want you to write Salammbô or he won't reply.'

I was amazed that this ratty ruse (because I regarded this whole show as only the latest of your many tricks) worked so well. The cute, trusting animal really did distract me, somehow subduing the turmoil inside my head. Let me hold him, I said.

'I'd be delighted to, babe,' you said cheerfully, passing Salaam to me with both hands, exactly as one would a tiny baby.

His fur was soft, his heart was racing and he smelled much better than I had expected a rat to smell—of woollen jumpers fresh out of the tumble dryer; and, when I breathed in his scent more deeply, of patchouli and peppermint.

For the next few days, whenever we didn't need to get dressed and go to the Triad, we spent our time on our mattresses, fairly monosyllabically, feet stretched out towards the other, and, one morning, we lay head to head only for two or three hours when I tried to ask you a few tentative questions.

Salaam, who had made his main den in the coal box of the old kitchen range, lining it with the hay I had put out, was allowed to move around the flat freely, but he liked being with you or me, especially in the evenings. And sometimes we let him stay, even through the night, because he was house-trained at astonishing speed, peeing and shitting in a very specific corner of the coal box, as far away as possible from his food, only nibbling at our covers and 'liberating' you from your watch, as you saw it, by gnawing through the leather strap while you were asleep, so gently that you didn't notice. Salaam liked nuts, biscuits, chocolate and games. He loved to take a run-up and jump onto my or your chest and then, eluding our grasp, escape and repeat the whole routine again. If he did get caught, he would squeak—with pleasure, you said. And he did seem to have a sense of humour; in any case, his squeaking sounded as raucous as a toddler's when it's tossed into the air and caught again.

Marlene had decided to stay away from us in future, justifying this over the phone with the argument that you hadn't given her a single answer, only excuses, but she did promise to take part in the final meeting. Juli, Clara and Hanna also dropped out, Hanna in the clearest of terms, Juli and Clara without any further explanation. Clara emphasized that she was also speaking for Juli and vaguely said they were sorry. They would come to the meeting, though, because, as Clara put it, they didn't want to 'screw things up' for you; you had been 'punished enough already'. But Frank stuck with us, saying that your fate interested him 'more than ever now, in particular as an artistic challenge, meaning on a professional level'; as did Marc who was the least worried of us all or at any rate didn't show his fear. 'It comes from my country, this shit. It comes from the States, like so much other trouble, and like me. Bet you the CIA's to blame, or NASA. They'll sort it out, though. They have to. But it's going to take a while this time,' he explained with a laugh, almost proudly, when he turned up late at night outside our door with a bottle of whiskey under his arm, unannounced and already slightly drunk, on the first Sunday after Joe had dropped his bombshell.

Although I was, with a few exceptions, the only one who now took you to the Triad or picked you up and had more and more frequently to accept that you were out and about on your own, and who arranged, cleared up and organized a lot of things, mostly for you, and sold flowers every weekend, I can hardly remember how this second month of group care passed; not quickly, in any case. Those of us who were left—you, Frank, Marc, me and even Joe—only discussed the absolute essentials, keen to be rid, I think, of the time pressure, the constraints and the control and to no longer have to play the child or the nanny, and we longed for the day when you would be entirely responsible for yourself.

Yet in my case, this longing was half-hearted. Half-hearted is, incidentally, the word that sums up best how I felt. I wanted to stay with you, close to you, but not too close. My fear of you and my love for you were at constant loggerheads; one would gain the upper hand, then the other, and overall this paralyzed me in a way I find hard to describe, numbing the pain and making the numbness painful. From head to toe I was like one gigantic molar that doesn't really hurt, but which you avoid biting with if at all possible. There were times when I was so full of despair that it made me rash. Fighting back my tears, I would fondle you and if this produced hard results, which it generally did despite the fearsome expression on my face (reflected in your wide-open, unhappy eyes as you looked up at me), I would put a condom on you and ride your cock which felt cool and faintly smooth, like a foreign body, like a dildo at first but soon as soft as a sausage; and that is exactly how it looked seconds after I had finally given up and rolled off you, partly because I was scared that the condom might have come loose with all my frantically inhibited movements and curled up inside me. Every time, though, the sheath was still on your . . . let me say 'penis', which looked abashed under the rubber and my pitying gaze.

During this period you were steadfastly gentle, submissive even, crouching beside my mattress in the dawn light, pushing the hair out of my face and kissing my cheeks and forehead in the belief that I was asleep. Sometimes you would even take off your dressing gown, crawl under the covers to me and use your fingers, albeit unsuccessfully, or simply snuggle up against me with your healthy-seeming, powerful body whose warmth just made me even sadder than I already was, while somehow comforting me too.

Enough. Fear is still fear, equal unto itself. It may not be completely meaningless, but it is totally pointless to bang on about it monotonously.

XIII

With the exception of Thomas, whom I never heard from again, and Christoph, who hadn't rung me since our second meeting but sent me a colourful postcard from 'Bella Italia' on whose back he'd written that he was leaving me the flower job for 'about four months' and wished me luck 'for the future', everyone else came to the grand finale with Joe, which you called the 'showdown'. Joe congratulated us and you; and if I'm not mistaken, he sounded a little sarcastic when he said that it couldn't have been easy to stick it out for so long.

After barely half an hour he declared the meeting over, and pretending to feel all emotional, you invited us to a 'very small party' at the Swan Lake Café, which even Joe agreed to. We were less than delighted by this news because no one wanted him to see through our pantomime at the last minute or just say he'd noticed what could scarcely have escaped him if he wasn't a total moron—and there was no reason to think he was. But Joe kindly went along with our act, spooned hot chocolate into his mouth, remarked that we smoked too much for him and, besides, he was tired, and soon left our not particularly joyous gathering.

Your 'ex-groupies', as you coldly referred to us, didn't stay long either.

Clara gave you two books as a parting gift, *Between Halflife and City Life* by a man called Dieter Panzer, and an anthology titled *The Fruits of Wrath*, which she highly recommended to you because three of her 'best poems' were 'immortalized' in it. And yes, Harry, I do remember much of what was discussed there, even the nonsense that Clara kept spouting, but I would have long since forgotten what those two publications were called if I hadn't inherited them, annotated with mean little sketches in the margins by none other than yourself, which shows that you had at least leafed through them, perhaps even read and kept them until the very end.

Frank gave you a four-colour lithograph, a portrait of you with empty eyes, arched eyebrows and a mouth almost forcibly twisted into a grin. That drawing has unfortunately disappeared; in any case it didn't fall into my hands.

Juli and Hanna gave you a quick hug before they left, turning their heads aside so only their hair touched your face.

Marlene, on the other hand, shook neither your nor my hand, gave a quick rap on the table and was gone.

Marc pulled a thick, coarsely knitted cardigan out of his ruck-sack, laid it around your shoulders and tied the sleeves under your chin. When he'd finished, he thumped your chest with his fist. 'There's bound to be another winter,' he said, laughing; and you and I laughed along.

As a rule of thumb, there are only four sorts of people: the good goodies, the bad baddies, the bad goodies and the good baddies. The good goodies and the bad baddies stay the same; there aren't many of them but they're boring. That's true of the bad goodies too. For a while they're the beloved children of upstanding parents with a little house and garden, but they grow up and want the houses and the gardens and do whatever it takes to come by what they think they deserve. The only ones who matter are the good baddies who get a bum deal the day they're born and, like the bad baddies, all they learn is to lie and cheat and fight and steal until they get a few years in the slammer and are on their knees or sometimes seek refuge in religion or ideology. They no longer direct their violence at others but at themselves, for fear of punishment and relapse, of becoming bad baddies, and spending the rest of their lives in and out of jail.

Within a week you had found an apartment, fulfilling your therapy's third-to-last condition. And since I knew it was the only option and that otherwise you wouldn't really be free, I took out a small loan and lent you the money for the deposit, which wasn't much because the flat, in the Emser Strasse on the edge of Neukölln district, close to Tempelhof airport and far from my own place, turned out to be a miserable hovel, a dark first-floor pit even in summer; and I could kiss goodbye to those few quid even more easily.

I was convinced you would end up back at my place sooner or later and that until then you would visit me every other day, if only to see Salaam.

It turned out to be more the other way round, though; I visited you as often as I could, given the photocomposition course the job centre had forced me to take and a growing lethargy that I dreaded as much as the disease. Sometimes I took a taxi in the middle of the night, hoping to surprise you, and I was glad that I couldn't ask you for permission beforehand because you didn't yet own a telephone. I slept badly without you by my side. I could hardly stand not knowing exactly what you were up to and convinced myself that I was only using up all that money because someone had to help you and that person was me, who else. Laden with household items, grub and bottles of red wine, with Salaam in one jacket pocket and cigarettes for you in the other, I would stand outside your door and ring the doorbell and knock until you let me in with a sleepy smile. You'd claimed that your property managers had only given you one key and that a second was 'on its way', but whenever I later enquired about this second key, you would talk about the need for written consent from the landlord which he would 'definitely' bring round soon.

As it turned out, I wasn't the only woman with an urge to help you. One evening, having just arrived, I was heading for the loo when, in your kitchen, I came across the red plush sofa that had once been Juli's spare bed. Yes, you said, she'd bought a futon and offered you this old thing.

What? I said. She was here?

'Nah, I was at Juli's,' you admitted quietly. 'Just quickly, hiya, seeya. I rang up a few mates right there and then from hers and arranged some transport.'

What kind of mates? I asked with genuine surprise.

'You know, mates . . . Some lads from the Triad and my karate club. You don't know them. Why would you?'

I couldn't elicit any more details from you and I wasn't in the mood to interrogate you further, although I did find it odd that you and Juli were in touch again and that you'd gone back to training and even had some mates.

You borrowed a drill from Frank and a whole load of tools, obtained a moving-in allowance from social services without my assistance, bought some second-hand lamps and some planks of wood from a DIY shop and worked away for days on end. As a lefthander who was all fingers and thumbs, I was of no use to you and would only get in your way, and I noticed that my infected-or-not-infected monologue was getting on your nerves quite a bit, however hard you tried to grit your teeth and put up with it. We had next to no common interests left, apart from Salaam and The Doors; you sawed and screwed together your 'new life as a free man', which to my mind was nothing but a free life as a dying man, and because I didn't know where I was heading, I was frightened of losing first you and then myself and of having to find a proper job again soon, and also that you might not pay me my money back . . . in fact, frightened of anything your sort would never think of calling the future, but my kind usually did.

A week later, about halfway through your final Triad month, you found a job via your probation officer, not as a typesetter because, as I knew from personal experience, there was little demand for those, but all the same in a printer's workshop, a small outfit in Schöneberg which reproduced old ad posters and billboards, 'the full range from Persil women and the Sarotti Chocolate's black-amoor through to the Erdal frog and Lurchi the salamander'. You said it wasn't exactly your dream job nor did it pay well, and you'd told a 'stunned' Joe that you'd rather be a 'drugs counsellor' because that was something you really knew about; but still, the main thing was that 'it had really taken the wind out of that arsehole's sails' and that your 'probation penpusher' had applied for 'the remainder of the sentence to be waived for health reasons'.

You were in a damn fine mood when I called on you that day, without Salaam and without any prior arrangement, in fact just to tell you how shit I'd been feeling since that morning, since I'd diagnosed myself as having flu-like symptoms that might, however, also be the first signs of an HIV infection. That's what I'd wanted to complain about to you and then let you reassure, if not console, me. But I didn't know where to start because you beamed at me, put candles on the kitchen table, uncorked a bottle of bubbly, placed a large bowl of yoghurt and fruit in front of me and said, 'Oh please, babe, wipe that latexphobic-dominatrix look off your face. Everything's great and you'll have your cash back by the end of next month at the latest. Haary's got this, you'll see.' It struck me again that you'd recently started pronouncing your name differently; when you talked about yourself in the third person, you didn't say Harry but lowered your voice and drew out the 'a': 'Haary'. When I asked why, you laughed deliberately loudly, which was also novel, and said this pronunciation suited you better. This strange argument would have been worthy of closer examination, but I was swept along by your optimism, especially as you introduced your 'latest acquisition'—a Sony record player that, you explained, one of your new mates had given you. You were just pulling The Doors' 'Waiting for the Sun' out of its sleeve when the doorbell rang several times. You looked a bit surprised, and I was a little annoyed, although I was curious to see which creatures might be seeking entrance at this time of night, as it was eleven o'clock and I'd never experienced someone I might not know wishing to visit you, neither at my place nor at yours.

You went over to the front door; I stayed sitting on Juli's sofa, heard three unfamiliar voices, a somewhat laboured one without any dialect and two Berlin-accented basses. And then there they were, standing in your kitchen, the Kling brothers, whom you nevertheless introduced individually to me, to my great and sceptical surprise, as I wondered by which features you distinguished them if you hadn't known them for very long or very well. Elmar and Eginhard, as you called them this one and only time—from then on exclusively as Elmi and Eggi or simply as the Kling brothers—were identical twins, the identicalest (forgive the false superlative) I'd ever seen. Did I ever tell you how freaky I found that? The Kling brothers weren't exactly dwarves, but they were small or, more accurately, short, and this was all the more striking due to their almost cube-like physique. Honestly, they looked as if they'd posed as models for Lego men; but unlike Lego, there was absolutely nothing round about the Kling brothers, not even their heads. Under their angular, somewhat unkempt Prince Valiant hairstyles they had angular, unexpressive but not stupid-looking faces, small broad hands whose fingers were all the same length, and small square feet encased, until they took them off, in chunky trainers with platform soles. Even the twins' movements and way of speaking were angular; you concluded your, or rather their, introduction with a completely apt remark that 'they're a little rough around the edges'.

Who knows why the girl I'd heard outside your door with the Kling brothers only came into view a few minutes later. She drawled something along the lines of 'looking for a tissue and forgot my tobacco' and sat down next to you on the couch with a deep breath. 'This is Lila,' you told me, 'but unfortunately I don't know her very well. Not yet.'

You passed your packet of Gitanes to Lila, who didn't think it necessary to add any words to yours; she took a cigarette, let you light it for her and inhaled deeply. Lila was thin and strawberry blonde, her complexion a pale bluish colour—I might also say light purple—and, other than her voice, everything about her was deep: her large, glistening eyes were set deep in their sockets, she had a deep dimple in her chin, deep cleavage and she sat huddled deep in the left-hand corner of Juli's sofa with a cushion clasped to her chest, as if she had taken root there.

As is only right and proper when visiting someone who has just moved in, the Kling brothers had brought a present: two sets of towels embroidered with different Mickey Mouse figures, each gift-wrapped and decorated with a rosette, one baby-blue, the other baby-pink, each set consisting of a bath towel, a hand towel and a flannel. I touched these things with a mixture of amazement and admiration; although extremely thick and fluffy, top-quality wares, they were, to put it mildly, horrendous, and I would never have thought it possible that these small but very virile-looking cubes would give a giant like you such a kitsch, girlie present. But after radiating abundant joy, you folded everything up tidily and put it back in the boxes and set them on their ends on a pile of planks, as if this were the place of honour for your greatest treasures.

You fetched out a bottle of Baileys, some biscuits, orange juice and Coke, and announced that the party could begin.

I'd never seen you as you were that evening. You kept laughing your new, ringing laugh, made fried eggs that only I ate, filled glasses, emptied ashtrays and, from time to time, asked the Kling brothers how so-and-so was doing and what such-and-such was up to, naming names that meant nothing to me because I'd never heard you mention them before. From the first scraps of conversation Elmi and the less articulate Eggi tossed your way—by which I learnt to distinguish them, as one was quite simply thicker than the other—I figured out that neither they nor Lila, even though she barely opened her mouth, were the Triad mates you'd spoken about but old acquaintances or even friends of yours.

The Kling brothers had done 'a few short years' with you in Seidelstrasse prison, Eggi for grievous bodily harm and Elmi, who had been released a month after you, for 'fraud and falsification of documents'.

You revelled in your memories: how you, one of the few 'Tegel inmates with a black belt' apparently 'knocked into shape all the flabby murderers' in the karate club, that only one of those arrogant political prisoners, old Till Meyer, had trained with Eggi and as a result become a 'top wrestler'. You talked about 'losers like Kalle, Ralfi, Hassan' and about Oleg, 'the old ladykiller with two left feet' who'd 'bitten the dust' so hard one day during 'Kata-Sahsi-Ashi exercises' that he knocked out both his front teeth. And sometime after you'd fetched the next bottle of Baileys from your seemingly bottomless stocks, you even tackled politics. Eggi cursed the 'Arabs'. Those 'dodgy southern fruits' were 'ruining business' by supplying people with 'shit' while also driving down prices. Elmi chimed in that that was 'small beer' and he was more interested in the 'wider historical context'; there was too much going on in the world and too little in Germany. 'They sit around, fondling their balls, blathering on about the peace the dear Yanks gave us, but then they go and do anything the Russians tell them to.'

Leaning back, totally relaxed, with your hand on Lila's drooping shoulders, you agreed with him: 'Yeah, what the hell are they playing at on their fat arses? They reckon thirty years of peace is something. Peace? Nice kind of peace, this Cold War. All I say to them is: we owe your whole weird truce to Adolf too. If he hadn't bitten off more than he could chew and our noses hadn't been so bloodied, we'd have been back bellyaching long ago.'

I couldn't believe my ears. Already pissed off, I drained my red wine in one and tried to intervene. Hey Harry, I began, didn't you say you were a left-winger? You should be glad . . .

'Shut up, we're talking,' you cut me off—in a scathing, authoritarian tone that was so unfamiliar and surprising that I fell into a stunned silence for the rest of the party, occupying my thoughts with a newspaper article in which a famous psychoanalyst described the phenomenon of multiple personalities.

It went on like this for some time. You told one another old-time stories about how you'd 'shafted' the 'fat jailer' X by nicking five litres of spirit vinegar from the canteen, and given Y a 'thrashing' . . . I lost the thread though; the red wine took effect. I also felt as if I was getting to know a Harry who had little in common with the one of my affections. And much to my amazement, which over the course of the evening attained proportions I can only describe as amazing, this Harry or Haary impressed me barely less than the gentle version you'd been for the past few weeks, who had in turn been unlike the one I'd run into at Winterfeldtplatz.

And I can also recall that Lila left the kitchen at one point and stayed away for about quarter of an hour, then leaned against the doorframe with a pasty face and moved strangely on her way back to the sofa, both lightly and heavily at once; like a floating bag, I thought. She ended up by your side again, rolled her eyes a couple of times and then slumped forwards, fast asleep, until the Kling brothers looked for and found their shoes and patted you on the shoulder and said that now they really must be going, and one of them—it must have been Eggi—loaded Lila, who was nowhere close to waking up, onto his back with his brother's assistance.

You said you needed some fresh air and went out with your odd mates and Sleeping Bag Lila. When you returned, which, if I remember rightly, wasn't straight away, you sprawled in your corner of the sofa again, yawning unrestrainedly, didn't put on any more music and started slurring and jabbering away: 'One fine Sunday morning, the snow had newly thawed, they picked up Lorentz and Peter, and put them in Zehlendorf.'

Although I was in a pretty bad state myself, I realized then that the only thing that had stuck with wannabe-proles like you from the whole ''68 hoopla' (your expression) were some slogans—and needles through which all kinds of substances had since flowed into you and accomplished some pretty comprehensive mind-expanding destruction. I could imagine that you were trying to get under my skin with your repetitive Lorentz-Peter sing-song, but I didn't imagine that Baileys, even two litres of the stuff—more than you'd drunk by a long chalk—could really have the same effect as alcohol, though maybe for once you really were pissed. In any case, I was pretty gone, but I made an impressive yet fairly ineffectual impression of the valiant missus, chucking glasses, plates and ashtrays into the sink with much crash, bang and wallop. Did I want to draw you into conversation? Would I have been capable of saying anything intelligible? Did I try to drag you off the couch and into bed?

What is certain is that I woke up late the next morning, too late for my photocomposition course, which had begun at nine, and was lying on your mattress alone. Still drowsy from sleep and maybe red wine too, I staggered over to Juli's sofa, but you were neither there nor in the toilet. For a few minutes I stood in my bare feet in your dark and dirty kitchen that smelled of mould and cigarette butts; I was choking on the tears welling up inside me and an urge to vomit that accompanied and threatened to overtake them. And although I sensed the worst, I reassured myself with the thought that there might well be completely harmless explanations for your absence, that you were buying bread rolls or cigarettes or had gone to the Triad. Anyway, none of that was of any help to me; I had to find a good excuse and go to my course because otherwise they would cut my allowances. So I bent over the pile of washing-up I'd built in the sink, washed my face with cold water, got dressed quickly and left your flat.

As I made for Leinestrasse subway station through a summer downpour that would at least provide me with an excuse for my lateness, I swore to myself that I'd spare no expense and move heaven and earth to make sure you had a phone soon so that I'd be able to keep tabs at all hours on whether you were home or not.

XIV

There were probably enough signs of the changes taking place inside you and then on the outside; to this day I couldn't say when they became impossible to overlook, because I managed to ignore them, against all reason and for as long as possible. Maybe I was too absorbed with my own worries about whether I ought to take a test or not, whether I really wanted to complete my apprenticeship and then waste away as a photocomposition specialist with Springer, or start some kind of studies instead, whether Salaam needed a mate or if I sufficed, whether you loved me or were just pretending . . . It was more of a process, a process that didn't exactly creep up on me, it even escalated towards the end, but it was not the court ruling that sealed it. It was like death, which no one and nothing, not even a machine, can clearly divide from dying because it doesn't happen abruptly and cannot be determined to the exact second; it doesn't matter what the doctor, who usually arrives too late, writes down in the register—and it doesn't matter anyway because dead is dead, even if death and the deceased look different after one hour than they do after ten hours.

And obviously you tried to hide from me what was going on. And of course I made do with your excuses. I didn't wish to see what, as it soon turned out, I couldn't see, meaning I couldn't *stand by and watch*; and you only forced me to do so once, and by lack of *foresight* more than anything else.

Yes, Harry, after I had made an urgent application behind your back and paid a very high one-off fee, you finally got a telephone, but I still didn't have a key to your place and you were no easier to get hold of, not for me anyway; you had of course discussed a code with your mates, as I eventually discovered: let it ring once, hang up, call again, let it ring five times, then pick up. And when I found out and didn't tell you and did the same the next time and got you on the line and could hear how stunned you were because you were expecting someone else, you all agreed on a new code.

I never found out when and how you started again, and whether it was heroin straight away; your notes offer no grounds for speculation on the matter and anyway, unless I'm mistaken, you didn't write anything in your notebook from August 1987 to March 1989. And when I asked you once, much later, when exactly your relapse had occurred, you said, 'That doesn't matter. It won't pay your bills', adding with a giggle, 'or mine.' Speaking of bills, you didn't sponge off me for weeks, not even after you lost your job with the Schöneberger advertising outfit while you were still in your trial period—so about a month and a half after you'd started—because, you said, your boss had found out about your infection.

Even though this information corresponded to my fundamentally fatalistic disposition, I silently doubted the veracity of your account. You'd always liked sleeping, but during that period you slept even more than usual, mostly with your eyes half-open, just the whites staring out at me. If I happened to meet you in your den, you were constantly tired, always dozing off, no longer reading fantasy novels or listening to The Doors, barely speaking, not even playing with Salaam. And I, idiot that I was, interpreted it entirely as the early symptoms of your illness, spooned noodle soup into your mouth and urged you to go to the doctor's, live with me again or at least swap this damp, foul-smelling flat for a better one. But you said everything was OK, you were just having 'too wild a time'. And when, as so often at that stage, I ranted and wept and refused to believe you were at karate training when you didn't open the door or pick up the phone, you admitted that you, as you put it, 'gave in' and invited me somewhat reluctantly to watch you 'but please not every time'.

At half past five the next afternoon, twenty minutes earlier than we'd agreed, I was waiting in a courtyard off Hermannstrasse in Neukölln outside an ugly flat-roofed sixties building with a crumbling scratch-coat facade; however, the Oyama Karate Club's open wooden door, through which not exactly daunting but nonetheless strapping lads went in and out in twos or threes, chatting away in Turkish or German, had been given a fresh lick of bright-red paint.

I felt a little uneasy since these men either paid no attention to me or, unless I was imagining it, shot me disparaging grins. I had already guessed that hardly anyone brought his girlfriend here, and I was afraid of inconveniencing you or, worse still, embarrassing you. I'd done what I could so as not to be mistaken for your older sister or even your mother, applying makeup, pulling up my curls into a 'pineapple ponytail' and putting on my smart new jeans, blue leather trainers and a baggy T-shirt with a bright neon print that was supposed to look cool and, more importantly, hide my not-very-sporty, chubby waist.

You arrived shortly before six, smiling, with outstretched arms and a canvas bag over one of your shoulders, which were always slightly hunched forwards. 'You look nice,' you said without a trace of embarrassment, and kissed me on the mouth with dry lips. We went inside, said hello to a beefy, ageing bloke who had gathered his long, thick hair into a kind of low bun and whom you introduced as 'Tarik, the greatest mechanic in Kreuzberg', and then the Kling brothers who were standing there, already changed into their kit. They looked even more identical and cubic in the square-cut white wraparound tops and baggy trousers that didn't reach their ankles.

I sat down with a few other people, all men, in perfect or less-than-perfect cross-legged or lotus positions around the edge of the wooden floor with strange curving and dotted blue, yellow and black lines painted on it, glad that I was still supple enough and not wearing a skirt.

You—that is, you and seven other men including Tarik and the Kling brothers—walked with an extremely dignified, upright posture into the arena, as I will refer to the theatre of operations, even though I found out long ago that it is actually called a dojo. In the white fabric, stretched perfectly taut across your broad shoulders, and the black belt tied around your narrow hips, you looked as smashing as you subsequently proved to be as a karate-ka. You all saluted the dojo with a quick bow and lined up in one row; you were standing next to a wiry Asian with tattooed arms, hands, feet and even face, who was fairly old compared to the rest of you and didn't appear to be Japanese or Chinese but more like Thai or Cambodian. He was the only one other than you who was wearing a black dan, albeit a wider one, and he shouted out something; I now know that this was the command 'sheiza' and I also know the other commands that followed on from this sheiza in the ritual. You knelt down, first left knee, then right, put your hands on your thighs and looked straight ahead at no one. The coloured man, obviously the highest-ranking master, called out 'Mokuso' and your eyelids closed, he called out 'Mokuso jame' and you opened your eyes again and bowed your heads to the Asian man who, as you later told me, was in fact Taiwanese; he had spent five years in Tegel with you for 'repeated drug dealing' and taught you during that time. You saluted him, 'Sensei ni rei,' then greeted one another, took your hands off your thighs, stretched them out a little above floor level, tilted your upper bodies slightly forwards and bowed again, your breathing audible this time. Only then did you stand up again in the same compli-cated fashion in which you had knelt down, bowed one last time and at last started to do some gymnastics and even a few exercises.

Oh Harry, I can't claim I had eyes only for you. Several others cut a fine figure, and even the Kling brothers didn't look quite as stupid as they usually did; but I couldn't help worshipping you. How high your feet soared and how safely you landed on them, how smoothly you twisted your hips, how accurately your arms shot out from your shoulders and how elastically your torso recoiled, and how powerfully you leapt into the air, twisted and extended your leg, seeming to float for several seconds above the ground. It looked as if you were dancing; and each of your opponents—you called them 'partners'—inclined his head respectfully as he approached you, and you bowed with even greater humility when he stepped back from you again, beaten obviously—you would say 'more experienced'.

Again I waited outside Oyama Karate Club for you, for almost another half an hour, and again you walked towards me with a weary grin, your hair still wet from the shower. I looked at you, as enchanted as if I were Titania, Lysander and Demetrius from *A Midsummer Night's Dream* rolled into one.

We went to my place. You didn't switch the light on, laid down on your mattress without even taking your sandals off and had no objections when I picked up Salaam, who immediately started to burrow under your covers, with the words, 'That's my place', carried him into the kitchen and closed the door on him after taking a couple of swigs of vodka straight from the fridge.

I was ready to forget everything, my only wish being to be with you, smell your occasionally acidic but now fruity breath, taste your slightly bitter skin, touch your broad, almost hairless chest, your powerful shoulders, arms and legs and your cock. I was ashamed of what I had done to it and for my panic, which might have been nothing other than cowardice, hypochondria and pathetic hanging-around in my already half-screwed and, in your absence, utterly eventless life. Eventless. Wasn't I fated to have 'less'? Was 'less' my lot? Did I have only one? Didn't I draw a new one every time we got together? And weren't even the duds top prizes in this particular lottery? Wasn't I always winning, even when I lost—first my fear of death, the next time my fear of that fear, then the fear of not being afraid, meaning that I was unprotected and, in that at least, like you, until we would be even more alike but no longer here . . .Via these kinds of thoughts, if that is what one can call psycho-polemical rudiments, fired up by three hasty shots of vodka and tearing around like tiny ferrets trapped in the darkness of my skull, I wound myself up into a—nevertheless heroic—fuck-you mood, which was far better than the sullen-sissy dog-in-a-manger paralysis with which I had plagued us for weeks. From now on, I wanted to love properly, selflessly, fearlessly. And who better to teach me than you, right? I wanted to hand over control and responsibility to you. I wanted to do some living at last—and you to be mine—with a capital L, like love. I never wanted to be small and cowardly again, and I wanted an orgasm.

You must have sensed that something was different or as it used to be, that the passion with which I pleasured myself with you wasn't fake. Your face brightened and, strangely, this made you seem more awake even though your eyes were closed. Your eyelids twitched, your lips softened and relaxed, as befitted their full and pretty shape. Looking back on that scene now—forgive me, Harry, for saying this—it's as if I'd found you in the snow and thawed you out, filled you with my breath and rubbed your arms and legs warm with mine; and you did come back, though not entirely. After a long struggle, I was rewarded for our zeal and had conquered my fear, but not you. Once again you managed to fetch me down from your pole, and your 'Pinocchio', as you sometimes called it, stopped lying in my pretty skilful hands.

'Don't be annoyed,' you said. 'For a sempai, the joy of being able to control himself is greater than joy itself.'

I found this phrase a little stupid, but nevertheless interesting enough, especially as the orgasm had dampened my euphoria. I asked you what exactly a sempai was and how long you'd been doing karate. You liked this subject and started raving on about how you'd been involved in it for ten years and how your talent had earnt you a whole lot of respect in Tegel. One day, probably with the Kling brothers, you would open a small studio, a karate school for boys over fourteen.

How come? I asked. Eggi started out as a wrestler, and his brother is a forger.

'Right,' you said, 'that's how Elmi got the cash.' And then you told me about Elmi Kling who wasn't as young as I might have thought and was, so to speak, our 'more learned' colleague, a qualified banknote and copperplate engraver who was also a master of every die-stamping technique and had had a 'trusted and fantastically paid job in the money-printing sector' with the Munich-based company Giesecke & Devrient before he was imprisoned. 'The kid's an absolute ace with the stylus—you wouldn't believe it. Along with two other guys, a printer and a reprographer, the two of us ran the printing workshop in Tegel, produced the prison paper, *Silver Lining*, and caused a load of trouble. Those were great times with Elmi.' The day after his brother was released, the 'otherwise idiotic Eggi', you continued, had organized a 'private conspiracy show' with the nice title of *Elmi's Secret Message* in a bar near the Oyama, 'only for well-heeled ex-Tegelians, really', but someone had a few collectors 'in tow'. You were there too, with Frank, who 'couldn't believe his eyes. And the art bods all right, you should have seen them; their monocles fell out in amazement and by the end they were almost fighting over the thing.' That same evening, Eggi had 'found a buyer' for every one of the three hundred or so stamps, 'some with an envelope, some without, but it was more expensive with. And now Elmi's got to grind like a port prostitute to deal with all the orders. He can't cope. He's already asked Frank if he can't help out.'

What do you mean, stamps? I asked. What's the trick?

And so you explained in detail that Elmi hadn't hidden the messages to his mates on the outside but had engraved and drawn them directly into the stamps with the finest needles dipped in a variety of inks. He'd produced a proper, numbered comic series, and they were obviously of great value to Elmi Kling fans as far afield as Japan. Of course, it was too 'brilliant' for the 'moronic censors to cotton on to' as they had settled for turning the envelopes inside out and deciphering the contents of the letters.

We laughed more that night than we have since; me, because you were laughing and you, about your great friend Elmi, four of whose envelopes, addressed to you 'c/o Eginhard Kling' and complete with the very cunningly and wittily doctored stamps from a 1986 Berlin series issued by the German postal service, you gave me a few days later and which hang to this day, professionally framed behind special five-times magnifying glass, between the two windows of my room; I consider them a sort of nest egg, because I've found out that they are now worth close to five thousand marks, although, or perhaps because, Elmar Kling died long ago. I don't know what caused his death or if his brother is still alive. A couple of years ago I was near Schierker Strasse, the address marked on the envelopes, and I weighed up whether to drop in on Eginhard and immediately found the totally dilapidated number 44, but his name wasn't marked next to the doorbell or on the letterboxes, neither on the ones in the front hallway nor on those in the hallways of the two rear houses, and the side wing had been sealed off by the municipal building inspectors.

XV

'High'; the expression still unsettles me. You may not be going anywhere, but the important thing was to feel that you were; never mind if it was a 'good high' or a 'bad high', the main thing was to be high. So you were 'on the needle' again, as it was called when someone was 'injecting', 'shooting up' or 'mainlining' opioids, preferably heroin . . . And yet you weren't *high*, you weren't even unwell, you were *low*, more and more under the influence of drugs with every passing day, maybe even since the time you took your last urine test at the Triad.

No, your behaviour wasn't unusual at first, no more unusual than it had been, anyway. You didn't do any of the things I read about later in handbooks—the kind for parents of children who might become addicts, for example. I didn't spot any prick marks or bruises in the crooks of your arms because it had been a long time since you'd been able to find any veins there and you mainly injected the junk into your groin; but that too I found out only later and not from you. I might not be particularly observant in general, but on the one hand it's more likely that I interpreted your withdrawn silence, your calmness, your lack of interest in yourself, in me, in the day-to-day, and your pretend or genuine fearlessness as your nature, and on the other hand suspected it. Your growing need to 'leech' onto me, as you called it when you snuggled up to me in the night, like a child, without any sexual desire, the cold sweat on your brow, the shadows under your reddened eyes, your disgusted poking around in the yoghurt and banana mush, a 'sports diet' which you sometimes made yourself, sometimes allowed me to prepare and then generally fed to Salaam or to me, the yawning spells, the micro-naps: I saw them all as symptoms of the disease. You could use whatever arguments you wanted—a tough training session, the heat, a bad mood—but although I didn't believe you, I'd pretend you'd convinced me or at least allayed my fears.

And your physical and mental state gradually stabilized, albeit at a low level, and you even became a little more active. Do you remember renovating my kitchen in late August while I was selling flowers in Halensee, or to be more precise, painting the sections of wall not covered by shelving, fridge or shower? I was happy, not because the stains had disappeared but because something else was still there, something you'd surely have discovered if you'd been more thorough.

I don't know what to say, Harry; maybe I can't really remember either, for reasons that finally need to be cited and for which I nevertheless need to psych myself up.

Throughout those summer weeks, although you were like a spider monkey at night, you seemed quite a lot more secure and mature, as if you were gradually coming to terms with life again. It's true that you went your own way, keeping your cards close to your chest, but when you did show yourself to me, opening your door or coming to visit me, you appeared steady and relaxed, almost serene. That may be why I complained less, but maybe I had simply learnt to suppress my fear better? Or was I just titillated by your inclination to sexual abstinence which I interpreted as an expression of a new direction, a newfound maturity, a change of mindset? In any case, I sometimes fancied it again, relying on the fact that you would protect me in the customary fashion. And indeed, you never turned me down, although never again did you take the initiative. I didn't take it too badly because something had happened—and that was not to be repeated either, even though I played more systematically and with considerably higher stakes later on.

Do you sometimes think back to my lottery win? Or bathing Salaam together in a salad bowl one Wednesday in August with the TV on in the background? How, as the numbers were drawn, the stupid expression about unlucky in love and lucky at gambling slipped my lips, and how suspiciously little I rejoiced? I no longer have to keep how much I really won that day a secret from you; not the modest sum of five thousand which I slapped down in ten five-hundred-mark notes on the table in front of your saucer-like eyes and took to the bank an hour later, but nearly eighteen thousand. Yes, Harry, with the lion's share—exactly twelve thousand seven hundred marks—I opened a savings account and kept the little book carefully hidden, wrapped in aluminium foil, in the same place where I stashed the income from the flower stall and other money I wanted not in my purse but within reach, behind the shower, between the cubicle and the wall.

You had your secret, and I had mine. Laugh if you want, call me a conflict-averse egotist, but it was the cash, and the cash alone, that gave me what I needed, distracting, comforting and calming me. In principle, I hadn't wanted to spend any of the money but to put it all aside, for later, in case you needed special medication that wasn't yet available in Germany, a convalescent stay or care, and the same for me, because I was counting on falling ill one day until I finally mustered the courage to go for the test, which, according to Joe, was only useful six months after the last 'risky contact' anyway; I'd rather have poisoned myself before it got to that point, but I couldn't even have got hold of poison legally and would've had to obtain it via some sinister and expensive channel.

Chance, for once disguised as luck, decided otherwise: I was able to do without benefits and turn down photocomposition jobs with Springer or elsewhere; the only work I continued was the flower business, and was even self-employed for a while later on. And yes, I took pleasure in going shopping for clothes and delicacies such as caviar, truffle oil and foie gras, which I tucked away in great quantities on my own and which soon ensured that none of the new sweaters, jeans, dresses and underwear fitted me any more; you got thinner and I got fatter and fatter. Which justified further extravagance. In a kind of frenzy, I leafed through catalogues, ordered cushions, bedclothes, porcelain and treats for you, both big and small: leather jackets, dressing gowns, pyjamas, slippers. I looted department stores and boutiques, sometimes quite literally; I began by slipping things into my pockets because it was a perfect distraction, a minor solace that was momentarily effective and actually quite thrilling. I told myself I was trying to please you, trying to create a cosy nest for us, but I knew it wasn't true.

I threw my lottery winnings away, which can't have escaped your notice, and you joyfully accepted my gifts, and even liked giving some yourself. Yet even during the relatively short period when we acted as if we were rich (and when I was actually far richer), you never asked for money, only once borrowing a hundred-mark note which you gave back only two days later, folded in typical junkie style, twice lengthways and then in half. To anyone else that would have suggested that you might be dealing again, but not to me, because it was only over time that I acquired all this boastful-sounding knowledge, for example the particular way of handling banknotes, the night sweats, the loss of appetite and reduced libido.

The Sunday you painted my kitchen ended in a row, our first real row, which I provoked. I confronted you with a choice, saying that I was happy about the white walls, but that you should have asked me and that I wanted my key back until you gave me one to your flat; the moment I had it in my hand, you could have mine back.

We should have realized that night, at the very latest, how little I trusted you, and you too would have had a reason to doubt my sincerity. Because I was naturally betting that you would never allow me unfettered access to your flat, and it was precisely the conspiracy that you had initiated and defended to the hilt that enabled me to do the same.

On Monday morning I woke up alone. My second key was on top of the fridge and beside it was a note: 'Blackmail is shit. Bye. —Harry'.

From then on we only saw each other two or three times a week; you were out and about, I was out and about. I contracted new vices such as going out to eat and travelling to Paris, Rome, London. I invited you to come along, but you didn't want to, using the fact that you had to look after Salaam while I was away as an excuse. And it was at your place in the Emser Strasse that our sweet Salaam took the final breath of his brief rat-life. You told me you'd taken him to the vet's, that he'd had something like distemper and they'd given him antibiotics. He died in your hands, 'without fear, peacefully, like a true Salammbô.'

I used the rest of the money—there was still something like seven thousand marks left—to buy into a flower shop in year two after you. Johanna, a qualified florist whose advert I'd answered, and I divided up the work in the small store on the corner of Ku'damm and Uhlandstrasse: Johanna two days, me three. She went to the wholesale market, I did the books—and in '96 we went bust; friendship over, money gone, bankrupt, up to our eyeballs in debt, on the dole . . . Never mind, I won't bother you with further details.

Then came that Sunday in late September when an old Renault 12 came barrelling towards Franz's stall. I jumped to one side in fright because it looked at first as if some overconfident drunk driver was going to crush all our blooms and greenery. But the car came to a halt a few inches from the flower buckets, the door opened and a laughing man stuck his head out and removed his sunglasses; that man was you.

'That surprised you, eh Soya?' you cried, hurrying towards me and waving a document under my nose. I took a good look at the folded rectangular piece of grey-green waxed paper, printed on both sides—and yes, with your standard passport photo, fluted and perforated, a blue stamp and two original signatures, it looked like a proper Class 3 licence, apparently issued on 8 April 1983 by 'Pol. Federal Driving Licence Printing Works 2935 Berlin 1.82'.

How does that work, Harry? I said. You were in Tegel then. Since when was anyone convicted of drugs offences allowed to take their driving licence? What's going on? And where did you get this old Renault?

'Trust me,' you said, 'I can drive. And the bit of paper looks great, doesn't it? The cops can't bust me with this. Tarik sold me the car for nothing. It's only temporary, until I find something better.'

I hadn't finished work yet, so you went off again to 'run a little errand'. An hour later you were back and chauffeured me home, via a roundabout route so that I could, as you put it, see for myself that you were 'a hotshot at the wheel'. You rested your arm casually on the frame of the wound-down window, the warm evening air ruffled my curls, the car radio was playing and the lights were on in Kantstrasse; I wanted to enjoy the whole experience, but I couldn't. As if I'd made a special request, I wept quietly to the sound of a song I heard only that one time but have never forgotten. 'Car crash / in a flash. // Straight in the ditch / son of a bitch. / Cops booked me / Guilty plea / Ever since / No licence. // Car crash / in a flash . . . ' sang a Turk in a cute accent and a monotonous, melancholy voice.

I asked you if the licence was Elmar Kling's work. You merely answered that I should 'stop blubbing' and not 'worry your head too much about it'. I was tormented by the idea that you were mobile now and that it would be even harder to keep tabs on you. However genuine they looked, your papers were bound to be fake and what you were doing right then was clearly a criminal offence. I closed my eyes and saw you, pumped full of dope in your karate outfit, with Tarik at your side and the Kling brothers in the back, racing through a rainy city I didn't recognize in the dark; sirens wailed, shots rang out . . . Harry, I said feebly, could we go and have a drink somewhere?

We ended up in a bar called The World's Lantern. You ordered a lemonade because, you said, you had to 'deliver me safe and sound, then carry on'. I understood that I was going to spend the night without you and so I got totally wasted.

A few days later, you really did disappear, for a whole fortnight. I was worried but not surprised, as I'd been banking on something like this happening. Or did you perhaps mention it that evening at The World's Lantern? I dialled your phone number several times a day and wondered what I should do and if I should look for you if you didn't reappear soon. But then, on Friday afternoon in the second week of October, you called up, cheery as you like, and said you'd been 'in Hamburg with an old friend to taste some real freedom'. When I rebuked you and wanted to know when we'd see each other next, you said your 'petty cash' had almost run out and you were 'ending it'. The terms 'petty cash' and 'ending it' rang in my ears for a long time afterwards; I could have exploded with helpless rage.

I just had another look at your driving licence and remembered how, three years after it came into my custody, along with your notebook, your passport and a few other things, I showed it to an ex-cop who lived downstairs from me but moved away long ago and may well be dead now. I told the old bloke, whose name was Karl Klawitter, that the document belonged to a friend and that I didn't know if it was legit. The former senior constable stood there in his doorway, looking slightly bemused, thinking perhaps that I was drunk again and was just pulling his leg, but he was then actually quite flattered; he pushed his glasses against the bridge of his nose and studied the document with all due care. Smiling, raising his right hand to his imaginary cap band, as if he had just carried out a traffic check and had no complaints, he eventually handed back your driving licence, pronouncing the following words: 'No doubt about it: it's genuine. As genuine as you or me.'

It's a shame, Harry, that I couldn't do anything with your 'bit of grey paper'; especially as I never had the chance to get one of my own.

XVI

Then came the day when everything changed again, but it didn't improve—and it didn't turn out as my hysterical imaginings had pictured it would. What actually happened was more banal . . . and more frightening, horrifying, terrifying? I can't find the right word to describe it; the ones I know are all too dull and blunt, like worn-out soupspoons.

Christmas and New Year's Eve had passed, two occasions that meant little to either of us; it was 1988. You came round to my place more often again; certainly not from rekindled love but simply because your ground-floor cave was freezing cold and too dark now, even for you.

On that Friday in mid-January, however, I waited in vain, even though we had agreed to meet up. It was snowing and had already snowed a lot the day before, and I had kept on calling your number until I finally managed to get through. You sounded hoarse, your voice constantly interrupted by coughing fits, when you said that your car engine was dead, your water pipes frozen and your spirits at rock bottom. Come over, Harry, I'll make you some noodle soup, I said to tempt you, adding sarcastically: Or would you prefer a hot water bottle?

'I can't, sorry. But I'll be there around eight tomorrow, babe,' you replied, coughed again and hung up.

It was Friday and well past eight o'clock; the noodles had been standing next to the stove for hours, soaking up my homemade beef broth, becoming ever softer, wider and paler, swelling up unstoppably towards the rim of my largest pot. I rang your number and let it ring, at nine, at ten, at eleven, at twelve; you didn't pick up. For a while I was angry and wondered, as this anger gave way to fear and I imagined all kinds of things—accident, arrest, run away, overdose—whether you'd perhaps already left your flat and were on your way somewhere, somehow, maybe in your knackered car, on icy roads, through the snow that had been falling incessantly since morning. Or on the subway? If so, you were bound to arrive in the next half an hour, and I could get my coat and intercept you in the five hundred metres between here and the station. But what if you rang while I was walking along Turmstrasse? I wrote two notes, stuck one on the door of my flat and one on the front door of the building and set off. The last subway from your direction on line U9, the only one you could possibly be taking, arrived at half twelve. I examined the faces of everyone I passed; that is, I tried to, but the snow flurry was so thick that I wanted to ask out loud: How about you? Are you Harry? I got to Turmstrasse subway station, chilled to the bone, my eyes watering, ran down the stairs and, positioning myself on the platform, watched the last train pull in and people get out; you weren't there. I ran up the steps again, hailed a cab, told it to take me to my house and wait, rushed into the courtyard, checked if the hallway light was on and, as everything was dark, ran back to the front door and added a sentence to the note stuck on it: *On my way to yours!*, crawled into the warm, snug taxi and gave the driver your address. We drove slowly and thus for a long time, passing two wrecked cars surrounded by police and paramedics, barely speaking because I wasn't allowed to smoke.

Since the door to your courtyard was never locked, I didn't bother ringing your doorbell but ran immediately to your two windows, from which there wasn't the faintest glimmer of light and would certainly have smashed them, had you not reacted to my knocking and shouting by pressing your palms to the windowpane and briefly showing your ghostly face, which I hoped was only distorted by the darkness, then you opened not your front door but one of your windows. I assumed that you'd help me inside; but when nothing of the sort happened and I couldn't even see you any more, I clambered over the sill, snagging my coat on the way in, tore myself loose, plopped down on to your kitchen floor, stumbled to my feet, switched the light on and, with bated breath, entered your room and approached your mattress. You were lying there, completely buried under three blankets. I fell to my knees beside you, called your name, tugged the blankets back a little, and caught sight of your hot, swollen face and—as you peered at me for a moment as if from afar—your bright-red, glassy eyes. I laid my left hand on your forehead. You groaned, probably because my hand was so cold; it was hard to tell if it had startled you or brought you some relief. I felt for your carotid artery; your eyelids twitched and your swaddled body shuddered. You had a high temperature and were wearing several T-shirts and at least three sweaters, all of them sodden, even the outermost. Shit, Harry, I said, what's wrong? Your only response was the sound of chattering teeth, followed by groans, a dry cough and an unsuccessful attempt to pull the covers over your head again. I went back to the kitchen, shut the window and looked around. Maybe, while you were still feeling OK, you'd fetched a few harmless drugs from the pharmacy—aspirin, cough syrup, maybe even a thermometer. I found nothing of the kind, grabbed the tolerably clean linen drying-up cloth which I tore in half, soaked it in cold water and went to wrap it around your calves; that's when my eyes alighted on the pile of planks and the two gift sets still leaning against the wall. In front of one of them stood a tin of citric acid powder, in front of the other a candle stump, next to which lay a flattened and empty piece of greaseproof paper and in front of that a bent spoon with a layer of brownish cotton wool stuck to it. That remarkable moment, when the utensils you obviously hadn't had time to clear away dispelled all the doubts I'd harboured at such expense, came almost as a relief to me: I was initiated; I had one foot inside.

A second towel was hanging on the back of the toilet door and I wet that one too and rolled it up to lay on your forehead because I didn't want to spoil the gift sets without your permission. I returned to your room with the three cloths and a bucket of water and tried to uncover your calves. But you thrashed about, moaned and pulled your feet up under your backside. You wouldn't stand for the towel sausage. 'Cut that shit out,' you groaned, 'I'm cold enough as it is. Come here instead and leech onto me.'

So I took off my coat and crawled in under the blankets, where it was like a sauna. I was amazed that one person could lose so much moisture, and whispered, You're sick. We should call a doctor. Maybe you need something before that, though? Honestly, Harry, if you'd asked me to do it, in that one moment and certainly never again, I would have cooked up under your guidance, filled a syringe and injected the stuff intravenously, and not just because I used to be an auxiliary nurse and had a taste for playing doctors and nurses.

'Nothing left. Eggi's only bringing more tomorrow. But whatever you do, no doctors, please babe.' Your answer came faintly and in bursts, and your breathing sounded like someone shaking a piggy bank.

Later, you fell asleep, tossing from side to side before settling down again, apart from the rattling in your chest. I must have slept a little too but was woken by your feverish ravings. 'I am András the Bear from Újpesti Dózsa,' you whispered ardently. I could've laughed because these words, which you repeated several times, sounded particularly odd coming from you, and I didn't know at the time that Újpesti Dózsa had been a Hungarian football club in the fifties and sixties; and I've been unable to establish whether an András ever played for them. But what I did see was that at that early hour you looked like anything but a bear.

A little later you lost consciousness; whatever I tried, you were unresponsive, just hot, maybe even hotter than before. I was seriously—and, as it turned out, rightly—fearful for your life, so I made an emergency call.

Within the hour I was able to open the door to the on-call doctor, a young African or African American. He looked at my tear-stained face with remarkable compassion, said, 'You need something to calm you down too,' ignored the chair I'd pulled up to your bedside and crouched down next to you. He looked up at me, because I was now sitting on the chair he'd rejected. 'It's acute pneumonia,' he said, taking a stethoscope from his bag. He requested my help, and together we undressed your limp body as best we could. He listened to your breathing and when he'd finished, he looked up at me again and asked, 'Junkie?'

I nodded and then said in a determined voice, as if I was only here to assist this doctor, Yeah, a long-term opioid addict, with hepatitis B and C and HIV-positive too.

A spark of excitement glowed in the doctor's eyes. 'Aha, now there's a combination we haven't seen too often. You know he needs to go to hospital right away? Please give me his passport and his insurance card, and pack the bare essentials.'

The bare essentials for a junkie? I asked.

The doctor shot me a slightly irritated look, but then he twigged and said, 'Oh, you mean *that*. You don't need to worry—your friend's coming to us at the Urban Hospital. He still needs a toiletry bag though.' He didn't pronounce the words 'toiletry bag' very fluently; realizing this, he gave a quick laugh. I laughed too but more out of relief, because the doctor would make sure you were OK. I put some underwear, your shaving kit, toothbrush and toothpaste in your sports bag, along with your papers, and asked if I could go with you. Only close family allowed, the young doctor said with a rueful look. 'And you two aren't married. Or are you? Cheer up, you'll be able to visit him soon. Here's a pill for you. And here's my card.' He gave me both and, lastly, his hand.

The ambulance drivers loaded you on to a wheeled stretcher and covered you with a sheet and a blanket that was woollen on one side and shiny on the other. I picked up your keys, accompanied your procession to the door of a white-and-red van parked directly behind your Renault 12, kissed your burning, cracked lips, and watched the tailgate close and you speed away down Emser Strasse, blue lights flashing, and turn left into Hermannstrasse and then stood there alone in the darkness until the sound of the siren had died away.

It was snowing, it was five o'clock in the morning—and I was so exhausted that I didn't go home and instead went into your flat and fell onto the mattress like a corpse. That morning was the moment I began to take leave of you, Harry.

You were treated in the intensive care unit for a whole week; I was only allowed to come and see you the following Monday. You were lying in a single room in the infectious diseases unit. The ward sister, with whom every person from outside the unit was required to register, instructed me to put on a sterile green bonnet and a similar coat. Thus disfigured, I entered your cell, because there is no other description for the narrow room with a small, high, tilting window through which at least a little daylight fell and which would, had I climbed on to your bed and stood on my tiptoes, have offered me a view over the bare tops of the staghorn sumac trees in the courtyard.

Your usual paleness had returned, perhaps with a slight yellow tinge. You were half lying, half sitting; your back was propped up against the inclined bed base, which was not very well cushioned by the mattress and the sheet. A thick tube had been attached with sticky plaster below your right collarbone, and through it an infusion was running into you, which, after greeting me with 'Hey, my little green monster', you described as your 'all-in-one solution for nutrition, salvation and consolation' because there was something in it that prevented you from 'losing it'; I didn't know if you knew how well I knew what you meant by that. I'd brought you a bottle of cherry juice, three of your fantasy books and the Kling brothers' light-blue towel set. 'Babe,' you said, 'where are the flowers? Or weren't you at Franz's this weekend?'

I couldn't have explained exactly why, but you seemed changed to me, as if you didn't fully understand what had happened. Your childishly high-spirited act disconcerted me; I sat by your bed, head bowed and silent, and only looked at you again when I sensed you were looking at me. Your pupils were as black and deep as holes; your look didn't attract me, but there was nevertheless something attractive, even magnetic, about it. It was—how can I describe this?—as if I were gazing not into your eyes but into all-swallowing craters. 'You're like most women, Soya,' you said. 'Strong men make you weak, but weak ones make you strong. And you want to be strong, right?'

Just then, the door opened with a creak; a nurse stepped between us with a cry of 'Excuse me' and set down a tray with a bowl of porridge, two slices of toast and a pot of tea on your bed-side cupboard. 'Let's get it over with,' she said, pulling on a pair of very thin, skin-coloured latex gloves in such a practised way that the words 'condom' and 'whore' sprang to mind, lifted your bed sheets, exhorted you to 'stay as you are, please', took a drawn syringe from a china bowl a second nurse who had suddenly appeared behind her was holding and injected its contents into the upper right quarter of your left buttock. As she rubbed the spot with a square of lint, she winked at me mischievously and said: 'That's the nice thing about people like your Harry—they love jabs.'

The cheeky nurse reminded me again 'not to stay too long' and wished us a nice evening. You said, 'They leave me alone for a while now', stretched out your arms towards me with a radiant smile, as if you hadn't been serious before, as if the words you'd said a few minutes earlier and which I, as I immediately proved, have remembered to this day, had never been spoken. 'Come here,' you begged in the same weak, almost childish voice, 'lie down next to me, just for a little while, until I fall asleep. Your Haary is already very tired.'

I hesitated, feeling a hint of disgust for the first time since I'd met you. I put it down to the smell emanating from you—or the blue fluid continually trickling into you, binding you to the umbilical-cord-like plastic pipeline and the soft, quietly gurgling pouch hanging from a gallows-like stand, which seemed to be a part of you already—or still? But I got over it and came to you. You were wearing one of those stupid smocks that are open at the back; I pushed my hand inside, touched your firm, warm, regularly rising and falling stomach and felt instantly so calm that I almost fell asleep as well.

As I found out from the attending doctor before my next visit, you had an unusual form of pneumonia, to be precise *Pneumocystis carinii*, and a fungal infection which he called *mycobacterium*; you had barely 600 T helper cells per microlitre of blood, and your liver was shrivelling up.

What are the prospects when Harry's acute symptoms subside, I asked.

'For him? Not very good. But very interesting for us,' your doctor replied with a smile.

XVII

'Very early one morning', as the partisan song goes, I was woken by the doorbell's insistent ringing; it was still pitch-black and there were no stars and no moon in the patch of window opposite me. And if I hadn't slept worse since you were in the hospital than I usually did and, in addition, hadn't been having bad dreams that morning or hadn't been there at all, who knows what would have happened.

They must have been making a racket for some time because I recall that it was a dark summer's night in my dream and the two of us were sitting, thirsty and messy, on a Mediterranean beach. The only sounds were the surf and the far-louder chirping of cicadas. Some of these insects flew past, just missing our heads; the beating of their wings created turbulence that cooled our faces, simultaneously menacing and pleasant, because there wasn't the slightest breeze coming off the sea. And one cicada flew straight towards us and for a few seconds I saw us reflected thousands of times in its huge, fluorescent composite eyes, you in the left one, me in the right . . . Eventually, however, it dawned on me that the intermittent noises didn't come from monster cicadas but from my doorbell, so I slipped on my dressing gown and groped my way to the door in bare feet. The people outside had heard something, had at any rate stopped pounding on the button, but their whispering and the tense atmosphere should have warned me, had I had my wits about me, that this didn't bode well.

What's going on? I cried.

'Hurry up,' a shrill female voice snapped back, 'there's a broken pipe!'

Still dazed, I switched on the light, unhooked the chain and opened up—to find myself staring down the barrels of three pistols. Next to the policewoman who'd fooled me with the broken pipe trick stood two male colleagues, one in civilian clothes and the other in uniform, both of them, like the woman, pointing their guns at me, and behind them were four more uniformed officers with truncheons. I didn't have time to adjust to this scene because three of the police officers barged past me, and the one in civilian clothing shoved me into the hallway, grabbed my arm and then the back of my neck so I had to turn round, and said, 'Now walk. No sudden movements.' After he'd pinned me against the wall, the order came: 'Spread your legs and put your hands above your head!' He frisked me from top to bottom, especially the pockets of my dressing gown, pushed back the sleeves and inspected the unblemished crooks of my elbows, returned his pistol to the holster under his anorak and reached for the back of my neck again. I was too stunned to say or ask anything.

Back in my room, I slumped down on to the still-warm mattress; the plainclothes police officer, whose hand was still stuck to my nape as if we were dancing a polonaise or acting out the fairytale of the Golden Goose, sat down beside me, stretched out his legs with a groan and muttered, 'Typical of you lot. Always live right at the bottom or right at the top, but none of you ever has a decent bed.'

The blond, slightly pudgy policewoman and two of the others shook down my room. They rummaged in drawers, the sewing box and the biscuit tin, rifled through the chest of drawers and the wardrobe, turned trouser and jacket pockets and handbags inside out, peeked behind the doors of the stove, ran their hands carefully over the spines of books, pulled pillows and duvets out of their covers and felt them—inch by inch, as meticulously as some women check their breasts for possible lumps.

After a while, I found my tongue again: Kindly show me your identification and the search warrant. And what were you hoping to find anyway?

The policewoman answered curtly: 'Search warrant? We don't need one when there's an imminent threat.'

Her plainclothes colleague, who let go of the back of my neck for a moment, said: 'You're not asking the questions here. We have a few first. Come on, let's sit at the table. It's better for writing the report.'

I could hear the other police officers banging around in the kitchen and pantry, so I said snarkily: Oh, great. I can make a nice pot of coffee for us all, if, that is, your comrades haven't tipped out the packet and poured the powder all over the floor.

'I like "comrades",' my guard said, 'and "powder" too. Now, down to business. How do you know Herr Rademacher?'

Rademacher? I had no idea who he was talking about.

'Benno Rademacher,' he added. 'And don't make out you're more stupid than you really are, you faded flower-power kid from the Near East. We found a notebook on Benno Rademacher's corpse with your name, address and phone number in it.'

I was dumbstruck and must have looked it. Then it dawned on me which Benno they might mean; it must be one who was with you the first time we met and ate asparagus with us the following Sunday. So that Benno, or Ben as you'd called him, was dead now, and his surname was Rademacher. I remembered his dense curls, his silver earring, the somewhat insolent and yet devoted way in which he carried on as your loyal sidekick, but I took pains not to show any of this because I could feel how attentively the man was noting my facial expressions and easily imagined that he could detect if I was lying or not.

There was this one guy once called Benno, yes, I said quietly. Ages ago. I bumped into him in the street. But I don't think he ever mentioned his surname, what did you say it was—Rademacher? He was Benno, full stop. But how come he's dead? And what do I have to do with it?

'That's irrelevant,' barked the plainclothes officer whom I now guessed must be a detective superintendent. 'Carry on.'

That's all, I snapped back. We went for a hot chocolate together and then, more to get rid of him than anything else, I scribbled my details on a serviette, unfortunately the correct ones, because otherwise I'd have had to think and he'd have been suspicious. Since the superintendent hadn't enquired about you, I didn't mention that you'd been with us or that I owed this contact to none other than you; but deep down I did wonder.

'Oh right,' the man said sarcastically, 'you were trying to get rid of him. Which is why you noted down in detail the number Rademacher could call you on and where he could find you if for some reason you didn't manage to pay your phone bill. Sounds logical, eh?'

By now the policewoman and her two colleagues had finished searching my room, and the other three came back from the kitchen, hallway and pantry. They shook their heads almost imperceptibly; one of them presented my savings book to the superintendent with a grin. He flicked through it and said, 'Tidy little sum. The kind of thing you need to keep well hidden.'

This finally got my back up. What a load of rubbish, I said, leaping off my chair, those are normal lottery winnings, which I'm sure you wouldn't mind having yourself, and they'll even stretch to paying the next phone bill. I can prove it. There's still a certificate from the German lottery fund in the savings book, if you fancy checking. And anyway: I've only ever taken money out, never paid any in.

'OK,' my interrogator said, 'that's enough for today. Please note here on the report that we have neither found, damaged nor taken anything with us. One copy is for you. I would recommend you keep this piece of paper handy and don't go thinking you're in the clear yet.'

I'm not signing anything, I said. First I'm going to see if your comrades have put the sugar back in the sugar bowl and the flour back in the flour tin and whether in general everything is exactly as it was before.

The pantry and the kitchen were squeaky clean; they'd even wiped the table and put three used glasses in the sink. I signed the slip of paper, escorted the whole bunch to the door, put the chain across, went into my room and smoked a cigarette. Then I had a quick shower, got dressed, pushed my savings book under a pile of records, picked up the bag with the pyjamas I'd bought you at Karstadt and locked the door three times behind me.

I opened the door of your hospital cell without knocking, stood in the doorway and, before you could say anything, said, Harry, your friend Benno is dead. I watched you exactly the way that superintendent had watched me.

'Benno?'—Both your gaze and your voice were once more very distant: 'Ben's dead?'

Yes, I replied, the police came today, six, with caps and all. One of them was going bald. I pushed the door shut behind me, sat down on your bed and told you what had happened, albeit not every detail and leaving out the bit about the savings book.

But why? I asked you. Why did they have to turn my whole flat upside-down?

'Oh yeah, I wonder what they might have been looking for?' You stared at me as if I had a screw loose. 'Your stash, of course. They were from the drugs squad, my little squirrel! Your name, address and phone number were in the diary of one of the earliest known junkies in the city, someone they fetched out of some toilet dead, rig still in his arm. They came to have a look-see if you were a customer or if he got the ingredients for his extreme unction from you.'

So you think Benno died of an overdose? I said. How can you be sure? Maybe he was murdered?

'Oh crap,' you said. 'Who would murder Benno? No one kills junkies; they take care of that themselves. Bit too greedy for his own good, our Ben. Could never pump his crown chakra full enough.'

Your smile was inscrutable, and it occurred to me, or rather it struck me, that you'd only ever mentioned Benno twice after that first Sunday you'd stayed over at my place, and both times it was me who asked after him. And on that evening with the Kling brothers, who must also have known Benno, the names of many prison mates had come up, but not his.

Sure, I said, you know best, after all they haven't hassled you. Why not though? Aren't you in Benno's notebook?

'Why would I be, lambkin?' you said. 'When my private secretary Ben copied your details into his book because you'd invited us and I definitely wanted to come and a paper serviette is easily lost, my most recent address was the same as his and he knew it by heart. And that night, remember, he vanished and since then it was as if the ground had swallowed him up.'

Harry, I asked, was Benno really your friend?

'Oh, dollymouse,' you said, 'I don't have any friends, only a girlfriend, and she's going to lie down in bed next to me now.'

On my way home I stopped off at a lawyer's whose name I'd found in the phonebook and called when the pigs left. I showed the lawyer the copy of the search report, signed by me and—completely illegibly—by the superintendent.

'Leave that with me. I'll take care of it. They won't bother you again,' Herr Raabe said.

It was true; I never heard from that drug squad superintendent or the homicide unit or any other special department again; and whether I now understand why or not, they'd never had their sights on you.

On 24 February, a week before my 42nd birthday, you were discharged from the Urban Hospital with a fairly clear prognosis. Your T helper cell count, said the doctor, had gone up slightly, but the disease had 'unmistakably and irreversibly' declared itself. However, he was 'almost more concerned about your liver' which was 'hugely damaged by years and years of chronic hepatitis'. He'd transferred you to the outpatient department, put your name on the 'priority list for a planned substitution scheme for serious addicts' and recommended 'in view of your fairly short life expectancy' that you apply for disability allowance. While I was cornering the doctor outside the nurses' common room and forcing him to give me information, you were on your way to the X-ray department; but I'm sure he was equally blunt with you. Still, I didn't let on to you that I'd confronted him and knew everything. In the subway I tentatively asked you what your plans were now. You merely grunted, 'What will be, will be'; you didn't 'fancy going on about all that shit', neither with me nor with anyone else.

No sooner had we turned into it than an icy wind swept along Emser Strasse, which looked as deserted as if, now that Neukölln's mutts would rather snuggle up behind the stove than go outside to play, only the passage of time was chewing away at it.

'Rain coming,' you said.

Give me a light, I said; and you put down your sports bag to strike a match inside your jacket. The pavement was dotted with a few frozen hillocks of old, soot-black snow, marbled with dog and human piss, and you put on a jolly face because in a minute you'd be 'sitting on my sofa, listening to a nice record'. I, however, was dreading your pit as much as the way you had said 'what will be, will be'.

XVIII

Oh Harry; you picked up again exactly where the pneumonia had stopped you, and with exactly the same things: dope and dealing. How else could you have afforded the Ford Granada, the 'super gas guzzler' which 'super Tarik' got hold of for you at the end of April? You were always cruising around the neighbourhood with the Kling brothers and Lila, but you visited me from time to time too and did something you never used to do, generally bringing cakes and your touching little presents, clay Buddha figures, porcelain horses and a little jewellery, presumably stolen. You were as greedy as you'd accused the late Benno of being, your pupils like pinheads the whole time, your gaze wavering, your sleep comatose. 'Why,' you said, 'would you want to watch me chuck up over the railings, especially now I'll soon be on a substitute anyway?'

And indeed they did 'integrate' you into their new methadone scheme, as one of the first HIV-positive junkies in Berlin, because you met the 'criteria', in fact you already displayed the 'full spectrum'. In theory, you were supposed to see your dose 'scaled back', 'gradually slipping out', as you told me, of dependence on methadone, which was after all only a different kind of highly potent substitute drug, but in practice you determined your own 'needs' and that you did so generously that there were 'a few drops left over for those poor devils without any official connections'.

You had to put in an appearance at your GP's every day and drink up your little cup's worth in front of a nurse, but on Fridays you received your, always copious, weekend ration in a screw-top jar to take home with you. You didn't want any other 'medicine' against the disease, not that any really existed, unless you had 'something acute'. For the period you were exclusively on 'meth', you felt 'totally lame' and flatter and more listless than you'd ever felt on heroin. And so you made your 'supplementary habit', which 'came about peu à peu because pure meth is so grim', into your 'main habit', quit the scheme, contracted your next bout of pneumonia and ended up back at 'Urban's' for the whole hot month of August.

The flat where I still live today had become available in the apartment block in Moabit—one room, kitchen, toilet, thirty square metres, second floor on the left. I sat on the edge of your bed at the hospital and begged you to please say goodbye to your hole in Emser Strasse and move into my building. 'So I'm back under your thumb,' you groaned. You'd grown thin and weak, but still looked like my Harry. Your doctor, the one we already knew, treated you as best he could. I stood surety for you with the Meyer Property Company, paid the deposit again, whitewashed the walls with Marc and arranged through Frank to borrow a car and transport your few belongings. You came home again and started up again exactly where you'd left off—until you could 'barely crawl', let your 'business slide' and asked me for 'two small notes' for the 'very last ten grams of dope and a bit of codeine and

Rohypnol to come down'. Even though you felt 'ancient', you weren't 'your grandma'; you didn't intend to 'push up the grass', especially as you could smoke it. It had all started with weed, and now you'd have to make do with hemp again, like those 'lemons with feathers' (you probably meant canaries), until 'the Grim Reaper sharpens his scythe and mows down old Haary—along with all the other blades of grass, the yellow and the green ones, the weak and the strong. He doesn't give a damn,' you said, smiling; the fewer reasons you had to, the more you smiled. You barricaded the entrance to your new flat with the three piles of wooden planks that Frank had given you and which were to be made into 'a bed, table and shelves some day'; I left mine for an initially indeterminate amount of time to a friend who had just arrived from the East, and rented, via Clara, a chalet in the Wendland that one of her comrades, a woman called Ilona Eisschädel from Freiburg, had bought during the anti-nuclear battles from a scared farmer but seldom used. It was ideal for our purposes, on a wood-land path, with the nearest bus stop fifteen kilometres away. We went there by train, laden with our three suitcases full of provisions, cigarettes and brandy for me, and then took a taxi to the gate. Should I tell you about the cold turkey?! No one knows better than you how terrible it was for you. My heart almost broke with pity, even though I scrubbed your shitty sheets in a zinc tub for seven days; still, after eight days you stopped raging and were able to drink quarter of a litre of camomile tea without vomiting it straight back up. After twenty days you'd turned the corner, after forty we went home, and in late November 1988 you relapsed and fell ill again, this time so badly that you never recovered. You spent Christmas, New Year's, January 1989 and half of February back at the Urban; a carcinoma had attacked your liver and you needed an operation to have the 'tiny' tumour removed, as you described it. Due to your HIV infection, however, they were unable to do radiotherapy on you or expose you to the stresses of chemotherapy. 'Still', your doctor said, 'your T helper cell count had plateaued at around 500 per microliter of blood' and you had a 'strong heart'.

I want to go to Spain. There's nowhere as beautiful as Tenerife. I imagine lying in the fine grey sand on Playa de Los Cristianos, all curled up like a viper. The sun is blazing down, and my flaky skin, which looks like the sand, is drinking in its rays. I'm alone, neither enemies nor prey anywhere near me. I don't have to move, in the daytime or at night. I can't hear anything, not the sea, no ships or birds, because I don't have ears or desires other than the desire for warmth. I can't get enough warmth or enough silence. Even if the sun were to go away, I would lie there, maybe bury myself under some sand as it holds the warmth for longer. But the sun doesn't go away, it just goes down. And tomorrow it will come again, and I'll still be here.

You never saw your small, bright flat in Moabit, the one I'd painted so nicely with Marc, again. They took you from the clinic to a brand-new project for opioid addicts who needed care and the first AIDS patients, run jointly by a number of social agencies. You were both and so you were one of the pioneers of the DIK, DIK being nothing other than the initials of Daheim im Kiez—'The Neighbourhood Home'.

The word 'Kiez' got on your nerves. Berliners had never called their neighbourhood 'Kiez', and this strange no-man's land into which you had now been banished was nothing like a Kiez. You were so right about that. I can recall every detail of my first trip there; the bit of land near Anhalt station was desolate and deserted. When the packed bus stopped to let only me out, I jumped off the running board at the last moment because I couldn't believe that this was the right place, looked around and thought: It's like just after the war; the ruined railway station, a half-built stretch of Stresemannstrasse, the Martin-Gropius-Bau covered with scaffolding and, a stone's throw away, the Wall of which nowhere else on the Western side offered such a stark view. In between, parched weeds and a few even uglier spots with pigeons, gulls or crows circling overhead. There were no other creatures in sight, no dogs and no humans; not a single soul to ask where Bernburger Strasse was. Eventually, however, I found it on my own although I'd walked past it three or four times, because Bernburger Strasse 9 A, B and C were not in Bernburger Strasse but in a gutted courtyard in Stresemannstrasse.

They'd given you one of the three rooms on the second floor, a good room with a large window from which, apart from the flat roof of a garage, one could also see the nearby church, the adjacent building plot and, farther away, an apparently unoccupied Nazi-era office block. You saw none of that, though, because the head of the new metal bed, which was obviously a permanent feature of the otherwise still-empty room, was under the window, or rather between it and the left-hand one of four walls painted a delicate shade of blue.

'Here's my little bear,' you said quietly as I came in. From that day on, you only called me 'little bear', never again 'babe'. I didn't ask how you were because I could see, so instead I sat down beside you on the bed where at least you weren't lying. You were wearing an ugly burgundy tracksuit that was much too big for you.

Army surplus? I asked.

'Private Krüger reporting back from dawn training. Permission to do another fifty squats?' you said with a smile.

We discussed which of your things you'd need and what you wouldn't for the time being. You wanted your clothes, 'but only the smart duds', and above all the dressing gown as well as the Sony turntable and the records, outdoor shoes, trainers and slippers, your fantasy novels and your shaver.

And furniture? I asked somewhat reproachfully. What about furniture? Or should I have Frank's planks delivered?

'They've got quite a few things here. Wardrobes, tables, chairs— all donated and nearly new,' you said.

And Juli's plush sofa? I asked with pretend horror.

'That can go back where I found it—on a junk heap in the street,' you replied, smiling.

And should I give notice on your flat? I persisted in asking.

'I think so,' you said and at last you'd stopped smiling. You wrote a power of attorney for me and explained that the project leader, a guy called Sören, had one too. So I didn't need to worry: if ever I couldn't bring you money straight away, you wouldn't starve. 'I'm tired,' you whispered in my ear and rolled over to face the wall. I understood: you wanted me to lie down alongside you; it was already our ritual.

We were quiet for a while, you stroking my arm and me your damp hair, before I asked: If you had a wish, just one, what would you wish for?

'Ten wishes,' you said without batting an eyelid.

To which I replied, as if to a child: All right then, let's make it simpler. Is there anything you're missing? Do you have a normal wish I can fulfil for you?

'Yes,' you said after a pause. 'A gun.'

I sat up and looked at you wide-eyed. Unfortunately, the drug squad didn't leave one behind, I tried to joke, but I immediately went back to being serious: And even if I wanted to, I wouldn't know where to get hold of one. And you really think I'm going to walk around out there, asking myself every minute whether you're still alive or have already shot yourself with my gift?

'You're right, that's a problem,' you said, smiling again now. My contacts aren't what they used to be either. And maybe I wouldn't even have the strength to pull the trigger. Think about it anyway, little bear. You don't have to give me the gun. I can pay for it.'

Oh Harry, you have no idea how often I actually considered this and wondered how much you might have been spared if I'd overcome my cowardice and got hold of a pistol.

I'd planned to visit you at least once a week, but I didn't manage to. Not because I didn't have time or because I was no longer bothered about you, but because you were breaking my heart; a different metaphor might be less kitsch but it would also be less true. Every time I saw you waiting for me with a smile on your face in that nicely arranged guesthouse for the terminally ill, holding your arms out towards me in your tracksuit or pyjamas, depending on whether you were feeling better or worse, and calling out 'There you are, my little bear', tears welled up in my eyes—and I usually couldn't keep them there. And you would pull me to your chest and say, to comfort me, 'Now don't be sad. Your Haary's with you' or something like that.

Might I have been less frightened by the ruination of your good looks and the erosion of your physical powers if the intervals between one visit and the next had been shorter? And if I *had* come more frequently and perceived these changes not abruptly but more gradually, I wouldn't have gained anything—in any case, I wouldn't have got you back. I had and still have a very precise mental picture of the Harry I loved and still love, and no subsequent one can replace it or chase it away. I measured everything I saw against that image. I felt like a customs official who looks up from an old passport photo at the—no longer remotely similar—face of the person standing in front of him and who can nevertheless tell if the person on the paper and the fifty-year-old who just got off a plane are one and the same person or not. Your image stuck (and is still stuck) in my memory. I saw that you were Harry but, unlike a customs officer, I was shocked each time, more and more, because your actual appearance matched the image less and less.

If such a thing existed, I'd love to have a hot-blooded snake, and it would have to be with me all the time. And bright orange curtains would be really great, although those might actually exist. I'd lie here, warming myself against my snake, and the light would fall through the curtains. Every day it would seem as if the sun was shining, whatever lousy weather they might be having outside.

I came whenever I felt strong enough again or when you rang up and asked where I'd got to, never with any remotely accusatory tone in your voice; both of these became less frequent with time. I would sit down by your bed, enquire about the tedium of your daily life and what you might need. Sometimes you had no wishes, apart from our ritual, but sometimes you did. You wanted your karate kit, 'a lemon to sniff', my red dressing gown 'but not freshly washed', a soft toy, if possible a tiger or a monkey, a helping of noodle soup, a cabbage roll, some vanilla ice cream and 'curtains the colour of the sun'; you never mentioned the gun again. On my next visit I would bring along what you'd ordered last time. Often you couldn't remember having requested this or that, but you still made a happy face and praised me for the 'nice surprise'. But you did really like the yellow curtains I put up over your windows with the help of your favourite nurse, Wolfgang; and now I've read your notebook, I know why.

I seldom stayed longer than an hour, partly because you became more and more monosyllabic from one visit to the next; 'as far as you were concerned' you barely had any need to open up, being, as you put it, 'lost in thought'. And when I asked you what kind of thoughts, you smiled and said, 'No idea.' Furthermore, you'd stopped smoking in September. 'It just doesn't agree with me any more. One drag and I start barking like a chained dog. Sometimes

I smoke in my dreams and wake up bathed in sweat from how sick I feel. I've even weaned myself off TV because Jogi sits there chainsmoking in his wheelchair in front of our one and only telly, as if he's parked in a drive-in movie and forgotten to leave,' you said; that was on one of your better days, a day when you spoke.

So whenever I wanted to smoke—and when didn't I?—I would leave your room and go either to the 'club room' to join said Jogi or, if he happened to be on duty, to your favourite nurse, Wolfgang. It was easy to talk to Wolfgang; he liked you and called you a 'real gent'. It was Wolfgang who told me how you really were. He reckoned you had not just a strong heart but also a strong character. Much depended on whether you were willing to put up with the pain you already had and the worse pain to come. That was the 'damn crux' with you junkies: it was almost impossible to relieve your suffering. 'People like you or me,' said Wolfgang, 'would be given opiates in his state, and everything would be cool. But for Harry, who's still on substitutes—for some time now Polamidon, which has less depressing side effects than methadone—morphine does nothing, not even at the highest concentrations. What can ease the pain of a life-long morphine addict if not morphine, the best pain-killer known to man? That's the question we ask ourselves here every day.'

I nodded and offered Wolfgang my pack of Camels. What do you think, I said as we smoked, should I bring Harry a small TV set and an indoor aerial soon?

'Sure,' Wolfgang replied, 'why not? Distraction is certainly good for him while he can still see.'

XIX

I need a chimney sweep, an arsonist and a weight to hold down weighty letters. Sophisticated demons . . .

Then came that October day when the East Berliners knocked down the Wall. Events had caught me—along with most Germans or at least we Berliners from both halves of the city—completely off guard, and I spent the next two weeks in a dazed state. My one-room flat in Moabit was like *The Night Camp in Granada*: an endless coming and going of friends I hadn't seen since '86. I can't say I was over the moon about this situation. My one and only privilege—having left for the West before the sudden end of the 'anti-fascist protection rampart'—disappeared with the Wall. I felt as if I was sitting in a train and all the trees I'd already passed were suddenly heading towards me again. It was exciting though; bottles of bubbly, wine, beer and brandy were handed around, and even people stupid enough to stick to water staggered around as drunkenly as the rest of us. During that time—you must forgive me—I barely thought of you once. I did however manage to drop in on you on 12 November, on my way to Checkpoint Charlie. I rushed into your room with two piccolos of sparkling wine. Harry, I cried, why aren't you at least watching TV?

It took me a second to realize that I was no longer outside but somewhere else entirely—and so were you. Your curtains were closed, and the light falling into your room with a yellowish hue blended with the light blue of the walls to form a dull lead-grey colour, while the few pieces of furniture looked almost black. Your room resembled a black-and-white photo with a pale-orange rectangle stuck on it.

You were sitting up under your bedsheets, leaning back on three pillows against the wall and shaking your head as you stared at your skinny right lower arm. I moved slowly closer and said, Hi Harry, it's me.

You looked at me, said, 'Oh little bear, I don't get it' and stared at your arm again. Show me, I said and now I could see two red marks that resembled large scrapes but couldn't have been. As Wolfgang later explained to me, a skin fungus your weakened immune system was powerless to resist was causing these outbreaks of eczema all over your body, 'tummy, back, legs, and—especially unpleasant—around the genitals.' We were now both looking at your arms in silence and outside we heard the hammering, shouting and helicopters until you whispered hoarsely, 'I know that piss artist Krenz is pulling the strings over on your side now, and Honecker and the border between the zones is gone, but I'm still here. I'd actually been planning that a West Berliner would die by the Wall for once, but it looks as if that won't happen now. Bad timing—either yours or mine.'

You fell silent again, and I burst into tears. I lay my head on your chest and wept, for you and for me, and because I'd fallen a little in love with another man, and because the 'Wallpeckers' were chipping away at my nerves, and because I realized how terribly weary I was. 'Come to Harry,' you said, and I cried myself to sleep on your shoulder.

When I woke up again, you were still sleeping, deep and fast. It was late evening; I picked up my bag, laid the piece of the Wall I'd brought you on the table and left, closing your door behind me.

On 11 November 1989, my path had crossed that of Urs Maiwald, the Swiss man I'd told you nothing about in the few hours we still had left together. Over the past year and in the last six months, when I already knew I was HIV-negative, I had let nobody, let alone a man, come near me. Urs I came to trust, though; he wasn't as handsome as you, but he was charming and observed the whole to-do he'd stumbled into with a mixture of curiosity and ironic distance. I liked his soft voice, his restraint and his candidness. Urs didn't pretend with me, and he wasn't into women. He liked women, he said, and if he really fell for one, he could even 'go to bed' with her on occasions. Urs was three years older than me, and a gardener by profession. His 'prematurely washed-out' parents, as he called them, had a few hectares of land in Allschwil on the southwestern outskirts of Basel; an orchard, greenhouses, a paddock. They sold their harvest of apples, pears and plums to nearby shops and distilleries and traded in a variety of exotic plants they cultivated under the glass roofs. Urs thought I should marry him so that his parents might finally 'retire with some satisfaction and transfer ownership of the farm to their son, now happily cured of his homosexuality'. Our deal was explicit—and advantageous to us both: he wanted the small operation in Allschwil, a 'nice companion with some idea of things' and a worker whose wages wouldn't be taxed because she was his wife. And I didn't want my

East German past to catch up with me, much preferring a Swiss passport; and of course, Harry, I wanted to be further away from you, although I wouldn't have admitted as much, even to myself.

When I paid you a visit shortly before my departure, I didn't manage to tell you that I was leaving Berlin and going to a different country. I said I needed some holidays and was heading to Switzerland for three or four weeks over the turn of the year. I really did believe that I would come to Berlin every couple of months, which is why I didn't give up my flat but passed it on to the same girlfriend I'd rented it out to while the two of us were in the Wendland.

That day—it was shortly before Christmas, and I'd brought you a large and not-very-teddy-like soft-toy bear—you felt pretty bad.

'Don't go thinking, little bear, that this chubby feller could ever replace you. Now have a nice time, behave yourself and don't forget old Haary,' you said.

We hugged, and I left. Wolfgang wasn't there unfortunately, so I gave the nurses my Swiss address and my phone number along with a large quantity of coffee, some sweets, a little bottle of brandy and—just in case you needed anything—two hundred marks in cash that I'd withdrawn from my account, not yours. I asked them to ring me without fail if your condition deteriorated or there was an unexpected problem. They promised to stay 'in touch' with me, and I was free, free for Switzerland but not from you; not that I knew that at the time, though.

XX

I saw you for the last time in person—in the flesh, as my grandma would have said—on 30 January 1990. I'd come to Berlin because I needed a few papers for my forthcoming marriage to Urs: a certificate of no impediment, a certified copy of my birth certificate, the document confirming my 'discharge from GDR citizenship'; and I also wanted to visit you, of course.

I got out at Kochstrasse subway station and continued on foot, looking around me. Potsdamer Platz wasn't yet riddled with craters and the ghostly silence that had reigned there hadn't yet given way to the noise of construction; but neither would it return and nor would the birds and the weeds. I wondered which of us two would better escape the imminent enormous changes, me in Allschwil or you here, although you were at the epicentre of the future. I'd left because I didn't want to be at home when Berlin dissolved, my East and our West, fearing that I too would dissolve and perhaps even disappear; I'd preferred to disappear somewhere else instead. I found it more normal to be a stranger in Switzerland than to become a stranger in two cities that couldn't stay the way they were, let alone go back to being the single city Berlin had once been, but would become something new, no one could yet tell what, but which, once completed, I might even like; not now though, not at the beginning; chaos spelled demolition, speculation and uncertainty. I could tell even from far away that during those difficult months most of us 'aborigines', whether East, West or Dual Berliners, felt like woodlice that had lived woodlouse-like under stones in an overgrown garden. But a great big hand had reached down and picked up the stones, and now the tiny creatures were scurrying around, spooked, or playing dead—and longing to have their homely stones back; darkness, peace and quiet, all the things they were used to.

You were sitting watching your mini TV, spooning a clear broth into your mouth. You seemed to be much better, and that made me happy. You beamed at me too, putting your healed arms around my neck before sparing a glance at the presents I'd spread out on your bed.

'Such a small country and such big chocolate bars,' you mumbled; your nose was stuck in a red cashmere sweater I was holding over your chest to see if it fitted. Cut it out, I said and pretended to take the sweater away again but, laughing, you protested, 'No, that's mine. It smells so wonderfully smoky, like you, little bear.'

Then came the news. The first pictures we saw showed the former head of state Erich Honecker, who had been arrested the day before. He was standing handcuffed between two police officers in a cashmere coat and his typical ushanka hat and staring defiantly, if not proudly, into the camera. Or into your eyes?

You underwent a peculiar transformation; as if in a trance, you laid down your spoon, which you'd picked up again, next to the Swiss chocolate bars and froze. I glanced back and forth between you and the TV. And truly, your eyes filled with tears, very slowly, until the water spilled over the edges of your eyelids and, drop by drop, ran down your gaunt cheeks. You didn't wipe the tears away; you wept in total silence. I'd never seen you cry and could hardly believe it. The pictures of Honecker had long since been replaced by images of arguing parliamentarians, yet still you wept. I reached for your arm. Harry, I said, what's wrong? Why are you crying? You shook my hand away, but you did let me give you a tissue.

'Don't you get it?' you said without looking at me. 'They're going to put him in the slammer again. But he's already done ten years, just like me. They wrecked his entire youth, he's sick and so am I. When he got out last time, his mates were in power and he became leader after "Goatie". He ruled over the people with an ex-con's distrust, knowing that a few of them had shopped him. But which ones? To be on the safe side he locked them all up, to punish them and take his revenge. When they finally let me out, I had to do that bloody therapy, but if it had occurred to anyone to put me in power, I'd have done exactly the same as him.'

I was too stunned by your longest and most unfathomable speech in two years to start arguing with you; and Wolfgang had told me on the phone about the toxoplasmosis episodes you'd suffered. Perhaps, I thought, your mind really has been damaged. How else could the fate of an old bloke who had tormented *us* for so long upset you so much? This incorrigible man had been ousted, sure, but he would soon be released, precisely because he was sick and frail, and spend the pitiful remains of his life if not in Wandlitz, then at least in the lap of a state of law. No, I didn't know then that a person's yardstick for judging is generally produced by the sum of their own personal experiences; that's another insight I owe to you. Unlike me, you hadn't seen the handcuffed Honecker as a toppled despot who was at last being held accountable for his acts, but as a fellow inmate who had to return to jail, and what he was going through was therefore worse than death for a former prisoner.

You died on 14 April 1990, two days after your 36th birthday, at 9.48 p.m.

Hounded by my guilty conscience, I'd rung the DIK on 12 April to congratulate you. Perhaps by chance, Wolfgang had picked up the phone. No, he said, I couldn't speak to you just then. You were too weak to get up. Your liver was in a critical condition and you had pneumonia and a temperature, such a high temperature that you surely didn't care what day it was today. They had considered whether to check you into the hospital, but you'd refused and also confirmed in writing: 'Do not resuscitate.'—'Come,' Wolfgang said. 'It could be very quick now.'

How much longer? I asked.

'I'm not going to make any predictions, but not long,' was his answer.

On 15 April I flew to Berlin and took a taxi to Bernburger Strasse. You'd already been 'taken away'. I cried and wanted to know where Wolfgang was and why no one had rung me the day before. 'Wolfgang?' said an unfamiliar female nurse with barely concealed scorn. 'He has a weekend off at long last.' He hadn't been 'informed' yet either, because he was only coming back tomorrow. But I would have to speak to Wolfgang anyway, because he had 'arranged the last matters with Herr Krüger'. In any case, she was new, hadn't been on duty yesterday and hadn't 'accompanied' you.

The next day Wolfgang handed over your handwritten will, designating me as his 'sole heiress', along with two full packing cases. 'Have a look to see what you want right now. The rest can stay here for the time being. I'll keep it for you,' he said.

When I asked him over a cigarette who had sat by your bedside and would be able to describe how you died, he answered, 'Robert, another new guy, a student, but he probably isn't coming back. He told me this morning after his night shift that Harry jumped into the Styx in pain but without hesitation. Yes, he literally threw himself into the arms of death.'

I put your will in my bag and gave Wolfgang or the DIK the little that would still be useful here: your yellow curtains, the record player, the TV, the bed sheets. Wolfgang had asked for them; I wouldn't have thought of it myself.

I picked up the things I hadn't taken with me in 1990 only a year later after the head of the DIK, Sören Arnold, had requested by registered mail that I do so, threatening to destroy the stuff otherwise. At the very bottom of one of the two packing cases lay your notebook, but I didn't read it until I finally set about unpacking everything.

For years I wanted nothing to do with your legacy. I couldn't bring myself to look at the faded pictures, the documents with your passport photo, Juli's necklace, the porcelain horses, the soft toys and the Doors records, to touch and smell your shirts, trousers, sweaters, dressing gowns, pyjamas . . .

Then, one day, shortly before the end of the millennium—I was long since divorced from Urs, and back in my flat in Moabit since 1992—I hauled the boxes down from the space above the dropped ceiling, took off my dressing gown, pulled on your moth-eaten red cashmere sweater, sat down on a cushion and began rummaging. First, I looked at the photos, the ones of you as a child, the ones of you and the Kling brothers, the ones of Salaam on your lap, the ones of the two of us outside the Karstadt department store in Moabit. I studied every page of your passport, your identity card, your qualified worker's certificate, inspected—with renewed astonishment—your driving licence, which even an ex-policeman had judged entirely kosher, and the fake leather case containing your postal bank card, two slips of paper with phone numbers on them, a few stamps and a wise saying torn out of some karate prospectus or a calendar: *By three methods we may learn wisdom. First, by reflection, which is noblest; second, by imitation, which is easiest; and third, by experience, which is the bitterest. —Confucius.*

And finally, to my not inconsiderable surprise, I pulled from a small slit I hadn't noticed at first because it was hidden under a flap between two compartments, a five-hundred-mark note, folded in typical junkie style, once across, twice lengthways. I looked at the red-brown note, caressed the dandelion and the beautiful caterpillar of the pale tussock moth nibbling at its leaves, then the gently smiling face of Maria Sibylla Merian, and remembered how you had once said that five-hundred-mark notes were your favourites; they were the only ones that gave you an 'almost erotic' sensation. I had been weeping the whole time, but now I wept even harder and, captivated by the sight of the delicate, fairylike insect next to the portrait of the artist, I wondered if this might be a sign, and if so, of what.

~

Nothing serious has happened since then; my life simply rolls on. When an opportunity comes up, I do some job or other, make myself a soup in the evenings and drink a bottle of wine. The lottery winnings are spent, and so is your Soya. I've tried with three or four other men and have had no regrets when they left me because, as the last one said, I was 'always so distant and dismissive'. I receive the dole and housing allowance now and I no longer diet. I was about to let myself go to seed when I read your notebook and discovered that I can talk to you and even write to you. I might take your five-hundred-mark note one day and find out what's so special about the stuff that separated us before death did, and from which you protected me as you did from infection. I've tried many things, but never dope. And if tomorrow or the day after I were to hear that I had cancer and couldn't be saved, your banknote would presumably cover a farewell fanfare. Until then I shall watch our film: we're lying on the mattress, head to head, barely moving, our breathing light. Your eyes are shut, mine look up at the open window . . . We have each other and time; nothing else, but lots of time, even if it no longer seems to exist.